The Silver Shell

A Romance Novel by

DEENA LOGAN

Dedicated to all those delightful people who have found
love when it seemed impossible.

And to the wonderful seniors in our world who continue to
make life worth living for themselves and their partners.

THE SILVER SHELL

by DEENA LOGAN

DAY-1

PREPARATION

DEBRA

Kim Dawson lay on her side on her parents' bed and watched her mother with concern. "Mom, what are you doing? I was talking to you."

Debra pawed gently through her jewelry case in an elusive search for earrings that actually matched.

"Honestly. One of these days I'm going to go through all this stuff and get it organized. Oh, here it is! No, wait, that isn't the one…"

Kim shook her head. "You heard what I said. I know you did."

"Yes, dear, I heard you. I… well, now… where on earth --"

"Mom! This isn't like you at all."

"Honey, I heard what you said. But you can see I'm trying to find this other gold earring. I want to wear them on the ship with my new blue dress. What is the matter with you?" She stopped suddenly. "Oh, my."

Kim quietly waited.

"Look at this. My goodness, I forgot that I had this."

"What is it, Mom?"

Debra lifted a delicate silver chain from which dangled a small silver ornament shaped like a spiral seashell.

"Look, Kim."

The younger woman propped herself up on one elbow. "Oh, isn't it lovely. Where did you get that? I've never seen you wear it."

"Your father gave me this years ago. I forgot all about it. I used to wear it all the time, especially when we went out. Then, I guess I just started wearing other necklaces and I put this one away."

"Dad?"

"Yes. He said there are real silver seashells out there, but they are very rare. And the person who finds one will find everlasting true love."

Kim's sad smile matched her mother's.

"I never heard of such a thing. I think your father made the whole thing up. He was such a hopeless romantic, you know. But this necklace is still special to me."

She handed the necklace to her daughter.

"It's really beautiful," Kim murmured. "So dainty."

"Why don't you keep it, honey? I'm sure Juan is your everlasting true love, just like your dad said."

They both laughed. Debra took the ends of the silver chain from Kim's fingers, hung it around her neck, and secured the clasp.

"It looks wonderful on you."

"Are you sure, Mom? You just said it's really special to you."

"I'm sure, honey. It's yours now. Besides, what use would I have for a silver shell at my age? And Tom would have loved Juan."

"You really think so?"

"Yes, indeed. He would love to have a son-in-law like him." She patted Kim's knee sadly, then playfully. "That Juan is a keeper."

"A keeper!"

"You know it. Well, I'd better finish packing."

Debra picked up to her jewelry box and went back to her quest for matching earrings.

"Mom, do you have to go now? I mean, this is kinda last minute and, no big deal, but I've got a wedding coming up soon."

"Oh, Kim, your wedding isn't for another six months. We've got plenty of time. And this really wasn't last minute. Your Uncle Paul and Aunt Becky have been after me ever since your father died to go with them on one of their cruises. They go on two or three trips a year and they always ask and I always say no. I couldn't see myself going on some romantic cruise without your dad by my side."

With a deep breath she put down the jewelry case and sat on the bed next to her daughter. Kim snuggled up and put her head on her mother's shoulder.

Debra gently took her hand. "Honey, I really don't understand why you are so upset over me going on a cruise ship."

"I just wish you weren't going alone. That's all. I mean... well..."

"Well, what, Kim?"

"Well, you're not all that young anymore. I'm just worried that something might happen to you. And there won't be anybody around. I'm scared, Mom. Okay?"

"Well..." Debra recoiled a bit. "I know I'm getting old."

"That's not what I meant." She tried to sound sincere.

"Yes, it is, honey. And it's okay. You're right, I'm not young anymore. Some days I feel a lot older than I am. But most of the time I feel pretty good. Which is another reason I'm going. In a few years I may not be able to do this. So I'm going to do it now. And I'm going to make the best of it. So there." She touched Kim's nose with the tip of her finger. "Besides, your Uncle Paul will be with me."

Kim smiled. "He's still the big brother, isn't he? I love that about him."

"Sweetie, I know you're concerned. And I appreciate it. And don't worry, there's plenty of time before you have to be a parent to me. But not yet! I've been around for sixty years. I think I've learned a few things in that time." She paused. "One thing I've finally realized is that I need to get on with life after your father. I think I'm ready to begin life as... as a widow." She smiled softly. "Besides, it gives me a perfect opportunity to fulfill his last wish."

Kim stroked her mother's hand and smiled as she lay down beside her.

"And there's another thing, too." Debra paused a moment and took a breath. "With you getting married, I'm going to be alone from now on."

"No, Mom, you won't be alone. You'll always be a part of our lives."

"I know that, hon. You and Juan will always be a part of my life, too. But… it won't be the same as your living here." Debra patted her daughter's cheek, then stood up and resumed pulling articles from her jewelry case. "Oh, look!" She held up a pair of silver-and-ebony hoops triumphantly.

"Oh. And here's that other gold one, too."

"Well done! Aren't those the ones Dad gave you for your twenty-fifth anniversary? You really want to take them on a cruise, where you just might lose them?"

"Now who's the old lady?" Into the travel case went the glittering earrings. "Look, honey, it's finally time to start this new phase of my life. I don't intend to be one of those old ladies who sit around all day watching TV, longing for the past and mourning their situation. I need to make some changes." She looked at the younger woman. "This cruise will be a start."

Kim stretched and sat up. "Seems like just yesterday Dad was here."

"Fifteen months and six days. But who's counting?" They both chuckled.

"I still expect him to come through the door any second."

"So do I, honey. So do I."

Debra slid a long silver necklace into the case and placed it in her luggage. She was ready to go, except for one last thing. She turned back to her dresser and gently picked up a black velvet pouch. Tears formed in her eyes as she carefully held it against her heart for a few moments, then placed it carefully in her carry-on bag. She looked at her daughter.

"I think that's it, Kim. I'm ready." She paused. "We have to leave really early in the morning. Are you sure you want to take me to the airport? You've never exactly 'done' mornings. I can always get a cab -- and I will if you keep trying to talk me out of going."

"Yes, I want to take you to the airport. Don't worry, I'll be ready. And I promise I won't say any more about your going. Except that I'll miss you."

"I'll miss you, too."

"But you can bring me a present."

"Well, of course. Now come here and give me a hug. You're still my baby, you know."

The next morning, Kim Dawson loaded her mother's luggage into the trunk of her sedan, then watched with a yawn while Debra buckled herself into the passenger seat. The sun hadn't quite risen yet. An early-morning flight was the only one she could get on such short notice. Kim climbed into the driver's seat and they headed off to the airport.

"Are you all right?"

"Yes, honey, I'm just fine. I really appreciate you getting up so early to take me to the airport."

"Mom, stop. I told you before I don't mind at all." She paused. "Any second thoughts?"

Debra smiled. "You promised not to bring it up. And no, no second… well, maybe a little one." She chuckled. "But I'm determined to do this and make the most of it. And I won't be alone, remember? It'll be fun to hang out with Paul and Becky. You know how entertaining she is."

"I know. I just wish Juan and I could go with you. That would be a blast."

"Save your pennies for that beautiful wedding. Besides, I'll be fine. What could possibly happen to a sixty-year-old woman on a cruise ship?"

"To a beautiful woman like you? Anything!"

"Don't be silly. Now tell me again, which florist did you decide on?"

They drove on into the early morning happily discussing the never-ending wedding plans.

At the airport, Kim pulled the bags out of her trunk and rolled them to curbside check-in.

"You need to tip him, Mom. Do you have a couple of dollars?"

"Gee, whiz, is that how it works? I ain't flown in a aeroplane since I was knee-high to a grasshopper."

"Right. There I go again. Sorry."

They stood on the sidewalk in silence for a moment. Kim's eyes began to water.

"Now don't you go crying," Debra warned. "It'll start me crying all over again, and I don't feel like putting another coat of paint on. I'll only be gone a week, for goodness' sake. And they have running water and electricity and everything on the ship."

"What about locks on the cabin doors?" Kim chuckled. "I know." She dabbed her eyes with a tissue. "You have the… um, pouch?"

Debra nodded. "Yes, it's in my carry-on."

They hugged a long time.

"Is Uncle Paul flying with you?"

"No. They flew down yesterday. We'll meet up at the pier. Now, don't worry. I'll be fine. I'll try to text or call you during the week, but if I can't, don't worry. There probably won't be a lot of cell service where we're going."

Her daughter nodded. "Okay. I'll try not to worry. Have fun. I'll be here next week to pick you up." They exchanged one more hug, then Debra watched her climb into her car and ease into traffic. One more wave goodbye, and she was gone.

She joined the check-in line and picked up her gate assignment and the claim tickets for her luggage. She was all set. She made it through security easily and bought a coffee at the only place open that early. She sat at her nearly empty gate sipping her coffee, watching people walk by. It was exciting to be out of the house and starting an adventure. But she felt so alone.

"What the hell am I doing?" she whispered.

FRANK

Frank Watson sat in the lobby of the motel, fuming. *That taxi to the pier should be here by now.* He'd flown into town the night before and gotten a room, just so he wouldn't be rushed in the morning. He'd packed one suitcase, a garment bag for his sport coat -- although he probably wouldn't need it -- and a carry-on bag with essentials. In his hand were two tickets for a cruise.

He snorted. *Why the hell did I bring both tickets?* His mind raced with doubts about this trip. A year's worth of planning and thousands of dollars later, here he sat; alone and discouraged, wondering why he was here at all. His wife, or rather his ex-wife, hadn't wanted anything to do with the cruise, but he couldn't see letting it go to waste. Now he was having second thoughts. Where was the value in an old man taking a romantic cruise alone?

Frank and Margaret had both enjoyed cruising over the course of their marriage. Each trip seemed to renew their love and re-energize their relationship. This one was supposed to save it. But that wouldn't happen now.

He jumped up as a taxi finally pulled up to the lobby entrance. The driver opened the lobby door. "Cab?"

"Yes." He stuffed both tickets into his shirt pocket and carried his luggage out to the cab. The driver loaded the bags into the trunk while Frank climbed into the back seat. Once the driver was buckled in, he leaned toward the back.

"Where to?"

"The cruise-ship dock, pier number seven."

"Just you?"

Frank chortled. "Yeah. Just me."

The driver engaged the meter and pulled out into traffic.

"It'll be about twenty minutes in this traffic. But you'll have plenty of time once you get there. First cruise?"

"No. We've... I've been on a few."

"You got a nice day for it."

The rest of the trip was spent in silence. Frank sat back and tried to enjoy the stop-and-go ride to the port. However, all he could think about was being alone.

"What the hell am I doing?"

"Sorry, mister. Did you say something?"

"It was nothing."

At the pier, Frank paid the fare and stood for a moment looking at the hordes of people coming and going.

"Well, here goes nothing."

He picked up his bags and headed for the entrance to the ship's terminal to merge with the masses.

Almost a year ago Franklin Leonard Watson had booked this cruise for himself and his wife as something special for their fortieth wedding anniversary. They hadn't made it that far, as long-simmering differences culminated in simultaneous affairs and then a shattering divorce. He'd wanted to cancel the trip altogether, but the tickets were non-refundable – tickets Margaret had acidly "given" him as part of the settlement. He had sought a travelling companion in his son, his brother, a close friend, et cetera, but finding someone who could get away for a week long cruise at the last minute had proved impossible. What was he going to do by himself on a romantic cruise ship filled with families and couples? Sourly he filled out his baggage tags.

He found the sign marked "Single Traveler/ American Citizen," the very last station at the far end of the counter. But, thank God, it had the shortest line.

He was alone in an enormous crowd. His disappointment descended into depression.

The line for single travelers may have been shorter than all the others, but there were still quite a few people traveling alone. Ahead of him were all the usual gaudily dressed retirees and excited single people who were obviously on their first cruise.

Then, well ahead of him in line, he noticed a lovely woman with long auburn hair, probably in her fifties. She turned her head and he was treated to a glimpse of her profile. Wait a minute; she looked familiar. Well, did she really, or was this just his loneliness wishfully thinking? She turned forward again and continued through the line without turning back around. He watched her make her way through the checkpoint and merge with the other passengers disappearing into the tunnel leading to the maze of walkways that would eventually deposit them onto the ship.

Frank shook his head. Running into someone he knew on this cruise was a million-to-one shot. What was he thinking? She was probably just some stranger who happened to bear a slight resemblance to someone he'd met before.

A sudden burst of obnoxious laughter from behind him captured his attention. He turned and noticed a middle-aged blonde laughing while she wobbled a bit. She was with two other middle-aged women, all cutting up with a man behind them in line. He was a good-looking guy, a little younger than Frank, very well-dressed and well-groomed. Somehow his manners didn't match his clothing.

As Frank gazed at them, the man happened to look up. He nodded and winked breezily, smiling back with big teeth. Frank's eyes yanked themselves back to the three women, noticing that they all carried plastic cups -- most likely loaded with a sweet alcoholic beverage but close to empty now. He turned away. *Maybe this trip won't be so lonely after all.*

He brushed the thought of them away as he cleared the checkpoint and entered the loading tunnel, suppressing the urge to moo.

SETTLING IN

By the time the ship cast off, Frank's suitcase had still not arrived, although the garment bag showed up almost immediately. A momentary fear of lost belongings gripped him. He stood on the private balcony of his stateroom, watching the ship slowly make its way out through the harbor. He liked this private balcony; he could see into the ones below him, but no one could see up into his. He smiled thinking that it was worth the extra money after all. As he looked around, it seemed as if all the passengers were outside watching the departure.

After the obligatory safety briefing concerning life vests and the assignment of lifeboat stations, he walked around exploring the shops, the pools, the bars, the casino, and the general lay of the ship. It was lunchtime and the buffet lines were open, but he hated mingling with crowds of strangers. He opted for the less noisy, more formal dining room. It would be a little more comfortable.

He was seated at a table for two and chose a light lunch: Caesar salad with a cup of tomato bisque. He looked across the dining room out the big windows and sighed gloomily. They had just left port and he regretted taking this trip. Although his ex-wife had told him he should go, he knew that she hadn't meant it. He had really come by himself just to spite her.

His soup and salad arrived and after surveying it suspiciously he began to eat. Food has a way of changing a person's disposition, and halfway through his meal he began to feel a little better. Spending seven days moping around this beautiful ship feeling sorry for himself was not a good plan. He decided he would try to make the best of it. Maybe he'd even send her a postcard.

Frank looked around the dining room at the various people. That's when he spotted her... the woman he'd seen ahead of him in the embarkation line was being seated just a few tables away. Her back was to him, but he recognized her lovely auburn hair. It seemed to shimmer. He smiled without knowing why. As she turned and spoke to the young waiter, he found himself staring at her profile. She was so beautiful. A light began to burn in his heart, a light he didn't understand. He had never felt anything like that before. *Must be the Caesar dressing. It was really too rich.*

But he was sure he had met this woman before, and it wasn't just wishful thinking. As she looked around the dining room in his direction he turned away to avoid her glance. Dying to find out who she was, the corny old pick-up line came to him. "Haven't I seen you somewhere before?" Frank shook his head. *How can I get away with a stupid line like that?*

He pushed his salad plate away and sat frozen, trying to work up the courage to approach her. He couldn't hear all that she said to the waiter, but he did overhear her introduce herself. Debra? Debra what? The name triggered a memory. Where had he heard it before? He watched her all through her meal, trying to connect that face with that name. It finally hit him.

"Good God, I really do know her."

EMBARKATION

Debra Dawson slid the dresser drawers closed and slowly surveyed the little cabin, checking for any items she hadn't yet put away. Tom had always insisted on unpacking at the start of each cruise, so they could enjoy the feeling of coming home after each day's adventure. He hated the idea of living out of a suitcase. After a year and a half, she still missed him. She smiled at his memory but ached from aloneness.

She had met up with Paul and Becky in the terminal before boarding but hadn't seen or heard from them since. She tried several times to contact her brother, but he didn't answer his phone. She assumed they were still getting settled in. Becky always over-packed for their trips, so there was always a lot of luggage to sort through and stow.

She sighed and stood up, absently smoothing her new slacks -- time to brave the dining room. Maybe she'd run into Paul and Becky there. Maybe the happy families and honeymooning couples would soothe her loneliness. Avoiding the mirror over the desk, she picked up her new white sweater from the chair, took a deep breath, and headed into the corridor.

The ship pulsed with the excitement of hundreds of passengers rushing along its decks. Nimbly she sidestepped the usual piles of luggage and parent-pursued children, pausing at the rail as a sea breeze fingered her long auburn hair. It was a perfect Embarkation Day. She turned to smile at Tom, but of course he wasn't there.

"Get a grip, girl." She pulled in another lungful of fresh sea air and went below.

In the attractive main dining room Debra settled into her chair, smiling faintly at the cheerful, harried waiter. He was young and reminded her of her daughter's boyfriend, Juan. As he greeted her she glanced at his nametag and chuckled. *Juan.* She wondered whether to share this little coincidence with Kim -- who just might not appreciate it.

"Hi, Juan, I'm Debra. How's it going so far?"

"Just great, how are you? Hope you're ready for a delicious first meal. What can I get you?"

"Oh, just a green salad, please. Dressing on the side. And maybe an apple. Going to take it easy today."

"Right away."

He smiled and walked away. Very cute. But, so young. Tom would've sent her his usual sardonic look between heavy eyebrows and the top of the menu. He liked to tease her about waiters, mail carriers, delivery workers. She missed that as much as she missed his strong arms and those sweet short kisses.

She shook her head to clear it and leaned back in her chair. The dining room was fairly empty. Most passengers were probably waiting in line at the buffet or gobbling hot dogs and pizza by the pool. She and Tom had always preferred the comparative peace of the dining room.

Her cell phone rang. "Hi, Paul."

"Hey, Sis! Sorry to miss your calls. We finally got all of Becky's luggage. It came in shifts. It's unbelievable what that woman packs."

Debra laughed, picturing him sitting regally on a pile of pink trunks and suitcases. "Where are you?"

"Still in the cabin. Waiting for Her Highness to finish unpacking. Might take the whole week." Paul chortled. "Where are you?"

"I'm in the dining room grabbing a light lunch. Want to join me? I can wait."

"No, you go ahead and eat. It looks like we'll be here a while." He paused a minute and she could hear him talking to his wife. "Becky says hi. We'll catch up with you later. I don't know how long I'll have cell service, so I may not be able to call you again. Where's your cabin?"

"I'm on the Venice Deck, One-twenty-two."

"Ok, great. One-twenty-two, got it. We're on Venice, too. If I can't get you by cell, I'll leave a message on your room phone. We'll probably run into each other, though. It's not that big a ship. See ya later, Debs. So glad you joined us."

"Okay, Paul. Look forward to seeing you guys. Bye." She hung up, feeling a bit more cheerful.

A young family caught her eye as they piled noisily around a nearby table. The parents, who appeared to be in their mid-thirties, studied the menu while placating two little girls and a dark-haired boy of about ten. Debra listened to their talk with amusement as Juan returned with her lunch. It looked very fresh and appealing, but she put her fork down after just a few bites. Maybe she'd just take the apple up on deck.

Two elderly men who seemed a little too well-groomed sat down at the table closest to hers, nodding politely even as their eyes slid over her face and figure. She tucked her feet under her chair and turned away to look out the big windows. They paid her no mind after their initial glance.

The ship was already out of the harbor and they were into their first day at sea. Seagulls flew nearby and occasionally landed on the water near her window. She felt the usual stab of envy: what would it be like to really fly free of the earth? She closed her eyes while the familiar darkness of loneliness surrounded her. She had been alone such a long time, maybe she should be used to it. And yet... Tom had been gone less than two years. *Tom.*

"Debra? Debra Dawson, is that you?"

The deep male voice startled her and abruptly pulled her back to the ship, something vaguely familiar to grasp. She opened her eyes slowly and focused on his face. It was attractive, unconventionally handsome, smoothly shaven and lightly tanned. Short, neat silver hair framed a broad forehead and strong eyebrows over prominent blue eyes that appeared to take in everything. Debra's glance lingered on his thin yet sensual lips, intrigued by the hint of familiarity in this face. She dismissed that notion; lately a lot of people looked familiar to her who weren't.

"Are you all right?"

"Yes, I'm all right, thanks. Do I... Sorry, have we met?"

"Mind if I sit down?" He took the chair across from her, smiling softly, not waiting for her approval. "Oh, yes. We have met. I'm Frank Watson. I'd be surprised if you remembered me, but we met a few years ago at a sales convention in Las Vegas. Your husband and I were on that panel about the new regulations."

"Frank Watson... yes, of course. I do remember you. It's so nice to see a familiar face. How are you?"

"I'm fine, just fine. But I'm a little concerned about how you are. You're a bit pale. I didn't mean to intrude, just thought maybe you were seasick. Is this your first cruise? I could offer a few tips. Is Tom joining you for lunch, or may I call him for you?"

"Not at all seasick, thanks. Tom and I have cruised before. This first day, with all the harried travelling, always melts me down. I appreciate the offer, but I think I'll just go back to my cabin and lie down for a bit. Thanks again."

She rose a bit too quickly and the room seemed to spin. Frank jumped up as well and reached out to steady her. His arm went around her waist and the other took hold of her arm firmly. She tried not to show him how grateful she felt for his strength.

"So sorry, I don't know what's the matter with me. I'm fine, really."

"You're very pale. Let me help you back to your cabin." He released her but stood nearby, concern filling his face, conscious of the stares from people nearby.

"Oh, no, I'll be fine. Thank you so much."

"Well, at least let me help you to the doors." He took her arm in his, escorted her to the entrance, and pushed open the heavy glass doors. "There. Hope you feel better."

"Enjoy the cruise, um, Frank. So nice to see you again."

He watched her step into the corridor, catching the door just before it closed.

"Would you and Tom like to join me for dinner this evening?"

"Dinner?" She stopped and turned back to face him, her gaze lingering on his comforting smile.

"Yes, dinner. You know, as in the evening meal." His smile deepened. He let the door close behind him and joined her in the corridor. "I like the meals they serve in the dining room but, being a single traveler, they always sit you at a big table with people - usually couples - who always want to know why you're traveling alone. If you two would join me, we'd get our own table. I'd at least avoid all those nosy questions."

"Your wife isn't with you?"

"No, she didn't make the trip." He glanced away and she caught a flash of irritation. Or was it perhaps sorrow? He looked back at her and forced a smile. "It's a long story. So, how about dinner?"

"I'd like that, Frank. Maybe later in the cruise?" Debra smiled gently, then turned and walked down the hallway without looking back.

"Of course," he called after her. "Well, give Tom my best."

He could only watch her walk away.

Debra wandered the ship aimlessly, lost in thought, barely noticing other passengers. Her lovely green eyes were mostly on the sea: calm, restful, a silvery blue of unknown depth and richness. Hard to believe that an infinite variety of fantastic creatures lived their strange secret lives below its shining surface. She wished now that she had taken scuba lessons when Tom had brought home the colorful brochures. He'd been very enthusiastic about it, but she'd put him off until they had more time. Tears pooled in her eyes, and this time she let them flow. She sank into a nearby deck chair and wrapped her arms around herself, resting her tired head.

She was dozing off when her phone rang and startled her awake. "Hello again, Paul. How's it going?"

"How you doing, Debs?"

"Good, thanks. I was just about to fall asleep here on deck. What's up?

"Wanted to give you our cabin number. How about we meet up for a swim and early dinner?"

"Oh, sorry, just left the dining room. I'm going back for a rest now, but I'll call you or come by when I wake up."

"Right. See you later, then."

She pushed herself to her feet wearily. Something somehow was missing: a strong comforting arm, blue eyes, that deep rumbly voice. *Now you're just being stupid,* she told herself as she headed down the stairs.

Back in her cabin she kicked off her shoes, opened the balcony door, and let the sweet cool sea breeze waft over her. With a yawn and a stretch she fell into bed. She cuddled a pillow tightly and was asleep within minutes.

Debra awoke with a start, shivering in the evening air and looking around vaguely. She stood up slowly and stretched and stepped out onto her balcony. She had slept a lot longer than she expected. She drew in the fresh air as if each new breath fed her soul. How bright the stars were! She thought of that sweet young family in the dining room, and of meeting Frank Watson. *Well, small world.* She took another deep breath, rubbing her arms briskly. She felt rested; she hadn't slept that well in a long time.

"Oh, Lord. Paul!" She picked up her cell phone, but there was no service. "We must be quite a ways out to sea by now." With one final sweep of the lovely view, she turned and went back inside.

The message light on her cabin phone was blinking. She listened to the message and then dialed his cabin number.

"Sorry to miss you, Paul."

"You must have bed sores by now."

"Ha, ha. Guess I was more tired than I thought."

"We've already eaten, sorry. Becky was starving. And you know how she gets."

"You bet."

"How about a nightcap?"

"Oh, thanks, but I'm not fit to be seen in public. Gonna shower and hit the hay. But I'll see you at breakfast, right? After we …"

"Yes, I'll meet you up on deck at dawn. Sleep well."

"Thanks. You, too."

Debra stood for a moment after putting down the phone, then meandered back to her balcony. She leaned against the railing for a long time, staring off into the blackness of the sea. The moon hung low on the horizon. There was no noise other than the sound of the ship slicing through the waves. *It's so peaceful. Maybe I'm going like being alone.* She gazed up at the stars and smiled.

She walked back inside, leaving the balcony door open so she could enjoy the breeze and the smell of the sea. She stripped, showered, and pulled on her favorite nightshirt. Tomorrow would be a new day. She climbed into bed and turned off the light. She snuggled up close to a pillow and sleepily took in the moonlight now bathing her cabin. Staring out the balcony doors, she sighed.

"I love you, Tom. But I want to live." She closed her eyes and slipped into dreamless sleep.

DAY-2

AT SEA

SLEEPLESS

Sleep eluded Frank. Lately his insomnia had become the norm. The older he got, the less sleep he was able to capture. He would usually fall asleep fairly quickly but wake shortly after. Sometimes he'd just doze on and off all night; other nights he wouldn't go back to sleep at all. The anti-anxiety medicine the doctor had prescribed him during the divorce hadn't worked very well, so he had chucked it. A cocktail or a glass of wine before bed didn't seem to help much, either.

He slouched in a lounge chair on his balcony wearing nothing but the bathrobe provided by the ship. The cool, night sea breeze was refreshing and comforting as it glided over his skin. A brand-new novel sat unopened on the table. Despite the thoughts chasing themselves around in his head, he found himself enjoying watching the eastern sky gradually lighten with the approaching dawn.

A knock on the door jostled him from his reverie and out of his chair. He admitted a waiter pushing a little cart with a pot of coffee and the selection of fruits, breads, butter, and jams that he'd ordered last night. The attendant set it on the coffee table, bowed slightly, and left.

Frank poured a cup of coffee, nibbled on a few strawberries, and returned to the chair on his balcony. The peace and beauty of this morning did little to quell the incessant thoughts racing through his brain.

"Goddamn Margaret," he muttered. "Two thousand miles away and she still haunts my brain. She's gone. Why can't I get her out of my head? Why can't I let go of her?"

By his second cup of coffee the sun had risen above the horizon and was painting his private balcony bright orange. He loosened his robe and felt the warmth of the sun envelop his body. It was comforting. He checked the time on his cell phone and set an alarm. "Ten minutes of sun, that's all."

When the ten-minute alarm sounded, Frank closed his robe and went back inside his stateroom. The sun had helped him relax and momentarily forget about his recent ugly divorce. He showered and dressed in shorts, sandals, and a loose-fitting Hawaiian flowered shirt – the perfect tourist outfit. All he needed was a stupid hat and a camera hanging around his neck to complete the look. He found a different shirt and put it on instead.

He hadn't eaten much the day before, and today's coffee and fruit hadn't hit the spot. He wanted a more substantial breakfast, so he was off to the dining room. *Who knows?* he thought as his stateroom door closed behind him. *Maybe I'll see* her *again.*

ASHES

With her hair streaming in the morning breeze, Debra stood on the deck as a lovely dawn broke before her. The red sun peeked over the peaceful peach-colored sea, its widening rays bathing the water and the ship in its glow. Such vast, eternal peacefulness slipping by. She gripped the rail for strength, enjoying the view for several minutes more. Paul stood beside her quietly, leaving her to the moment.

It was time.

She reached into the large canvas tote at her feet and drew out the black velvet pouch. Pressing it to her bosom, she closed her eyes and murmured a few words. She kissed the pouch and took her time untying the strings. She held the pouch up and slowly turned it over the railing, watching the sea breeze carry Tom's ashes toward the rising sun.

It had taken longer than she had imagined, but now it was finally done. He was gone. The clean, cold, blue-gray water had accepted his remains, and his final wish to have his ashes distributed into the sea had been fulfilled. She brushed the velvet pouch gently against her cheek a moment longer, then put it back in her tote.

Paul put his arm around her shoulders. "Tom was a great guy, Sis. And he sure loved you, Debs."

She nodded silently.

The sun was golden orange now, beginning to blaze as it lifted clear of the horizon. The morning was warm and full of comfort. She leaned against the railing remembering the many years she had shared with Tom.

They stood quietly for a moment until they heard a slight rumble.

"Wow, Sis. Guess I'd better feed you."

"That was you, not me!"

"Come on, let's get some breakfast."

"Is the dining room open this early?"

"Probably. You go ahead and get us a table. I'm going back to the cabin to see if Becky is up yet. If you don't see us in fifteen minutes, then we're not coming."

"Wait a sec." She gave him a nice long hug. "Thanks for getting up so early and being here with me for this."

"Thanks for including me. I wouldn't have missed it for the world."

"You're the best brother anyone could ever have."

"I'm the only brother you have, so that's not saying much." Paul squeezed her tight. "I'll see you later on. Maybe at breakfast, who knows? Take care, Sis."

She was pleasantly surprised at how crowded and noisy the dining room was. Juan waved her over to her same table. As she passed the young family she'd seen yesterday, one of the little girls suddenly jumped up in front of her and squatted to pick up the doll she had dropped. Debra stopped to help her and was rewarded with grins and greetings from the parents. She smiled back and patted the little girl's shoulder.

"My name's Annie, what's yours?"

"I'm Debra."

"My daddy says you're very pretty for an old lady."

"Annie, you hush, now," said her embarrassed mother. "Sit down and finish your breakfast."

"I'm so sorry, Miss Debra," said the young father. "My wife caught me admiring you yesterday, and, well, sorry…" He broke off, blushing to the tips of his ears.

Debra laughed. "No apologies, please. At my age I'm just happy to be noticed."

Their friendliness lifted her heart as she moved on to her own table. The two elderly men paused in their conversation to wish her a polite good morning. She nodded and smiled at them. There was something unusual about those two impeccably dressed guys. She was about to stop at

26

their table for a chat when Juan arrived to put coffee and juice down and to hold the chair for her.

"What's good this morning, Juan?"

"Everything. Feeling hungrier today?"

"Starving. How about a spinach omelet and one slice of dry whole-wheat toast?"

"Just what I had in mind, Debra." He smiled at her and rushed off to the kitchen.

She sat back to enjoy the room and the sun on the sea. The day opened before her like a golden flower. The air seemed soft and clear, all the colors around her more vibrant than before. A delicious breakfast was set before her in no time, and she knew she would savor every bite.

She was gazing out to sea when she realized that someone was standing by her table.

"Oh, good morning, Frank. Sorry, I didn't see you there."

He smiled. "You looked so peaceful and I didn't want to interrupt. I just stopped by to see if you were feeling better today."

She smiled back at him. "I certainly am, thanks. Must've been all the excitement yesterday."

"Yeah. Traveling is such a nightmare anymore." He stood there, looking down at her awkwardly. She could think of nothing more to say, but again noticed how attractive he was. Should she invite him to sit down?

"Well," he finally said, "I'm glad you're feeling better. I'm sure I'll see you around the ship. Looks like a beautiful day at sea."

"Yes. You, too."

He took a few steps away, then, after a second thought, suddenly returned.

"I hope you don't mind my asking this, Debra. It's none of my business, but are you traveling alone, too?"

She seemed to blanch in the sunlight, then said quietly, "Yes. Tom passed away about a year and a half ago.

27

He... he wanted me to bring, um, his ashes -- " She choked back the rest of her sentence and brought her napkin up to her eyes.

"I'm so sorry. I had no idea."

"It's all right."

His awkwardness increased. "Again, I'm sorry. If there's anything I can do --"

She smiled up at him, her emerald eyes liquid. "Thank you, Frank. I'm really okay."

He nodded and walked away to his own table without looking back at her. She watched him go and thought that he seemed genuinely embarrassed for intruding on her grief. *How considerate of him.*

Throughout breakfast she couldn't help but smile a little as she occasionally glanced over at him and caught him looking at her. At one point, she turned and looked directly at him while he was staring at her. Their eyes locked. His blue eyes were so deep, so alive. They were pulling her into them.

LIZARD

Despite the awkwardness of that conversation, Frank had enjoyed speaking with Debra and could see that she was feeling much better. She was so lovely. He wished he hadn't put his foot in it by asking about her traveling alone. He felt embarrassed and flustered for prying into her grief. Not knowing what to say, he excused himself and crept back to his table.

The hunger that brought him to the dining room had abated. He ordered toast and a soft-boiled egg. All through his meal he couldn't keep from sneaking a glance at Debra out of the corner of his eye, studying her when she wasn't looking in his direction. He guessed her to be in her fifties. He didn't know why he was so captivated by her. She wasn't movie-star beautiful, or cover-girl gorgeous, or runway-model attractive. However, she radiated a natural, wholesome beauty, especially this morning without any apparent makeup. Her green eyes set above slim cheeks seemed to speak to him. Her well-formed lips, neither thick nor thin, pulsed a healthy pink without lipstick.

She glanced over at him and he held her eyes for just a moment. Her smile could melt the coldest heart.

His gaze was suddenly interrupted.

Strolling, or rather sauntering through the dining room was that boisterous man who'd been behind him at the check-in station. This was the same guy who'd been cutting up with that noisy bleached blonde and her friends. Women would think his type was handsome, Frank supposed. Normally he wouldn't have given him a second's notice, but the guy was impossible to miss. He wore powder-blue linen slacks and a bright red flowered shirt with the top few buttons open. A cream-colored linen sport coat, the sleeves pushed up to his elbows, burgundy loafers without socks, and a matching belt completed his outfit. It wasn't really a terrible combination of clothes, but on him it just looked bad. Frank shook his head and thought that a guy who looked that good should get some help picking out clothes.

Covertly he watched the man move through the dining room, leering at all the women he passed. He was so obnoxious, he couldn't take his eyes off him.

"Oh, no." The guy was looking directly at him and heading his way. He considered getting up and leaving the dining room before this lounge-lizard reached his table, but he had just gotten his food. He was hungry. And trapped. He concentrated on his plate and hoped the guy would just pass by. But no such luck.

"Not bad, huh?"

Frank looked up. "Excuse me?"

"Not bad." He gestured toward Debra. "The babe by the window." He pulled the chair out and sat down across from Frank. "I saw you talking to her. She's a looker, huh, buddy? Yeah, I was checking that one out myself. A little older than I like 'em, but you never know. Say, I like your shirt. Silk?"

"Excuse me?"

"Is it silk? If not, it's a real good fake."

"Look, uh… Mister…?"

"Sorenson. Dave Sorenson." He extended a hand, and the rings on his fingers cut into Frank's skin. "Industrial machinery sales. Big stuff, you know? Boring mills, turret lathes, you know, things like that."

"Look, Mr. Sorenson…" Frank began, dropping the man's hand as soon as possible.

"Dave. Call me Dave. Yep. Work like a dog about six or seven months a year and then take the rest of the year off and let loose. Right, man? I do some traveling, see some sights, do some partying, and score me some. Ya know what I mean?"

"Dave…."

"Do any good, yet?"

"'Do any good'? What are you talking about?"

"Well, I saw you in line yesterday, by yourself. And I thought to myself, here's another guy on the prowl. Another party dude."

"No, Dave. I'm not a party dude, as you suggested. And I'm certainly not 'on the prowl."

"Okay. Well, hey, I guess you do what you do. Each to their own, right? I always take cruises. Never had any trouble finding a good time on a ship, know what I mean?"

"No, I don't. Dave." Frank looked down at his food. "Now if you'll excuse me…"

"I didn't catch your name."

"Oh. It's Watson, Frank Watson."

"Nice to meetcha, Frank. Now I gotta tell ya, I make a pretty good stack selling those machines. But that don't pay for this kinda lifestyle. No way. I got me some good investment advice a while back. Making money like you wouldn't believe."

"Dave!" Frank raised his voice just enough to interrupt. "I'm trying to enjoy my breakfast here, and I don't mean to be rude, but I really like to eat alone… and in peace."

Dave shrugged and stood up. "Sure. Sure. No problem. I usually don't do breakfast myself. I'm waiting for the pool bar to open. That's where I get my breakfast -- two whiskeys over easy." He laughed out loud. "Look, about that investment advice, the guy who gave it to me is a multimillionaire. You seem like a good guy. I'd be glad to talk to you about this amazing opportunity. Guaranteed big returns on a meager investment."

Frank let out a long, disgusted sigh, tossed his fork on the table, folded his arms across his chest and frowned blankly at Dave.

"Okay, no problem. Maybe later, huh? I'll catch you around the ship. It's not like you can leave or anything, right?" He guffawed again, and people in the dining room turned to stare. He leaned in to Frank. "I just got one question, man," he whispered loudly. "You got something going on with that dame there, or not? I mean, if ya do I'll back off. I don't want to go muscling in on your turf, if you're on the make with her. Know what I mean?" He chuckled and lightly chucked Frank on the shoulder.

Anger was building in Frank. He wanted to punch this joker, if for no other reason than the demeaning way he was referring to Debra. But he controlled himself. Instead he just shook his head and looked away.

"Great, man. Wish me luck."

Frank watched as Dave walked by Debra's table, purposely bumping into it so he could apologize and strike up a conversation with her. He watched with anger as the guy pulled out a chair and sat down at Debra's table. She laughed a few times during their conversation and seemed to be enjoying his company. Frank's appetite was completely gone now. He could feel his face getting flushed with anger... or was it green from jealousy?

HER DAY

The big breakfast made Debra sleepy. She had intended to get in a good hike on the running track encircling the upper deck; now, however, all she wanted to do was take another nap. Having gotten up early to welcome the sun on the rear of the main deck and release Tom's ashes to the sea, she didn't want to go back to bed so early. She walked out around the pool and considered an early morning swim, but it was already too crowded and too noisy. She wanted a little more relaxing atmosphere.

She smiled at her trip so far. She had already met a handsome gentleman who was an acquaintance from years ago, and a very good-looking salesman who appeared to be quite well off. He dressed a little funny, but he was charming in a weird sort of way. Maybe this trip wouldn't be so lonely after all.

She glanced around at the crowd and couldn't help but notice that the salesman who had introduced himself to her at breakfast was sitting at the bar. He couldn't help but stand out. She smiled recalling their brief discussion. He was charming, and she was flattered. *What was his name? Dave, that was it. Dave Something-or-other.* For a fleeting moment she thought about going over to him to say hello, but she reconsidered, thinking that would appear too forward. She didn't want to give him the wrong idea. *Although, why not?* she thought. She was a consenting adult and he certainly was … interesting. For the first time in years, she thought about sex.

Smiling, and blushing, Debra turned and walked out of the pool area remembering that the ship's brochure mentioned an adults-only pool on the same deck as the health spa. She decided to find that pool, hoping it would be more conducive to her state of mind.

The adult pool was not very easy to find, perhaps by design. She had to travel through the spa, down a hallway, and then through two unmarked doors. It was not as crowded as the main pool, but she had forgotten that age eighteen is considered adult. A group of young adults, whom she thought of as kids, occupied the pool with their shenanigans and laughter. Again, a swim at this point would be more of a challenge than a relaxing endeavor.

Debra wandered through the mall of duty-free shops and then walked around the various restaurants crammed into the same section of the ship's main deck. Most of them were themed, like seafood, or BBQ, or Cajun. Some were more ethnic, like Mexican, or Japanese, or Italian. None of them really appealed to her. Once past the restaurants she came to the end of the hallway that emptied into one of the two theaters on board. The marquee announced that tonight's show would be a showcase of Sixties and Seventies musical performances from various old performers from that era. She shrugged. *Well, it'll be something to do, anyway.*

Debra figured her wandering around the ship was as good as a hike around an exercise track. She returned to her cabin and reclined on the bed to relax before lunch. She stared at the ceiling, trying to follow the various thoughts in her head. She thought about this morning and the men she had met. Dave was cute, charming, but much younger than she was. *So what's wrong with a younger man?* She thought about Frank, also handsome and charming. He was more in her age group. She felt like a teenager having two boys competing for her. Her final thought before falling asleep was the deep blue eyes of Frank Watson. She let out a giggle and finished with a sigh, smiling at the thought of being captivated by those eyes.

Debra's nap was far from relaxing. She never truly got to sleep. She would fall into that dream state and be startled awake by a vision of Tom or some other memory.

She got up and changed into her swimsuit, anticipating some sunbathing and a possible dip in the pool. The clock read two in the afternoon. Had she really been in bed that long? Even though she had missed lunch, she wasn't the least bit hungry. She pushed open the slider to her small balcony and breathed in the fresh sea air.

A breeze engulfed her and tossed back her hair. She smiled at the sensation. She stepped out onto the partially sunlit balcony and leaned against the railing again. Tom had loved the sea. She bent forward to see the ocean being cut open by the bow of the ship. Tom's face smiled up at her from the ocean waters and she felt the warmth of his embrace. That loving feeling of his hands on her body suddenly exploded in her. She closed her eyes and welcomed the memory of his touch, his lips on hers. She saw his eyes… but no, his weren't this piercing blue. She gasped. Whose eyes were these?

HIS DAY

After breakfast, Frank went to the concierge desk to ask about the shore excursions he had purchased in advance. He, of course, purchased them for two people, but now he was the only one. The concierge sympathetically explained that shore excursions were booked through third parties and completely non-refundable. There was nothing he could do. Great, Frank thought, another thing his ex-wife cost him. Now he was stuck with a companion ticket for shore excursions and no companion. Perhaps Debra... but, no...

Days at sea were boring to Frank. It would be different if he had ever learned to relax. He returned to his room and changed into swim trunks and sandals. Ruefully he changed the silk shirt for the flowered one. He stopped at the health spa and sat in the hot tub for half an hour. It was so soothing that he thought he could fall asleep in there. He probably would have if it weren't for two women continuously chattering about their grandchildren.

He left the spa and walked out around the large pool on the main deck. It was late morning and the sun was already too hot for him; at his age he had to watch how much exposure he got. He found an empty table in the shaded area by the lounge. He ordered iced tea and watched the girls sunbathing and the families playing in the pool. He hoped he would see Debra Dawson around the pool area, but she wasn't anywhere to be seen. He would have liked to see her in a bathing suit... or maybe a bikini. She had the figure for it.

He felt tired after his tea and returned to his stateroom. With a rocky sleep the night before, he decided to take a nap before lunch. He removed his sandals and shirt and collapsed on the bed. He was asleep within minutes.

When Frank finally woke from his nap it was the middle of the afternoon. He had missed lunch. He was bored. He checked the ship's itinerary. They were to dock at their first port early tomorrow morning. He opened the door to his balcony and let the sea breezes fill his stateroom. The balcony was partially in shade, so he sat out there in his swim trunks and began reading the book he'd brought with him, a crime drama from one of his favorite authors. It opened with a love affair on a tropical island that went sour. Frank closed the book. *Too close to home.*

He stood up and moved to the railing, staring at the open sea and then around at the various balconies below him. Most were empty in the middle of the day. But there was one balcony where a young lady was stretched out, sunning herself in her lounge chair wearing a very skimpy bikini. Frank felt a hot twinge race through him, his mind filled with a fantasy about her.

It had been quite a while since Frank had been with a woman. He had cared quite a bit about his wife, Margaret, and always enjoyed making love with her. But those times had gotten fewer and farther apart. She was too busy, not in the mood, not feeling well, didn't have time... the excuses piled up. Over a year ago, a chance meeting with an old girlfriend, another disappointing rejection from his wife, and a little too much to drink had led to a one-night sexual encounter. Frank had felt guilty but glad about it. Margaret found out about it through a friend of a friend of a friend, and it eventually led to the divorce. During that six-month court battle, Frank found out about Margaret's affair with a coworker, an affair considerably longer and more involved than his one-night stand. His guilt about that night vanished.

Frank watched the sunbathing lady and was dreaming up a fantasy about her when a movement on another balcony on the lower deck off to his right caught his eye. *My God, it's her!* Debra had walked onto her balcony wearing a one-piece swimsuit. Her figure was a perfect shape. She leaned over the railing to look below. His reaction was strong and immediate.

The rest of the afternoon was a blur for Frank. He killed time in the casino, the bar, his room, the shops, and just walking around. He chose to forego a sit-down dinner and grabbed a burger and a beer at a poolside snack bar. He couldn't get Debra out of his mind. Why was he obsessed with a woman he'd only met the day before? His reaction to seeing her in a swimsuit had pleasantly surprised him, but he chided himself for wanting her so much. The woman was in grief over the loss of her husband. He couldn't figure out this burning desire for her. He had never felt this way about a woman in his life -- even as a teenage boy with raging hormones.

The sun began to set. Loving couples wandering by now stopped on the deck to watch the setting sun, holding hands or hugging each other. Frank sat at the table in the poolside snack bar observing them. He didn't like to admit that he had always longed for a relationship like that.

It was obvious to him that Debra was a loving, caring woman. When he first saw her at that sales conference with Tom, he was impressed by how much the two of them were so visibly in love. Now she had come all the way out here alone just to distribute her husband's ashes to the sea. That was the kind of love he had been dreaming of his entire life. Dreams didn't always come true, at least not for him.

Frank checked his watch. It was six-thirty and that musical revue from the Sixties and Seventies would begin in an hour. He had time to kill, so he ordered another beer. He'd see the show and then go to his stateroom for the night. He was looking forward to the first port call tomorrow if for no other reason than just to get off this ship.

SHOWTIME

Debra reclined in the shade of her balcony, watching the endless sea drift by. She sat in deep thought and remembered her life with Tom. It was a happy and fulfilling marriage. He was a doting father to their only child, Kim, and a wonderful husband, a kind, loving, and gentle man. Until he got sick. The cancer was brutal. She spent the last two years of his life caring for him every waking minute of the day and night -- so much so, she had neglected caring for herself.

She looked at her nails as she sat on the lounge chair. She had never really paid much attention to them, at least since he got sick.

"What a mess."

Back inside her cabin she looked at herself in the mirror. Not a cursory look; this time she studied her reflection. Her dry, shapeless hair with its streaks of gray, her sagging cheeks, the small worry lines around her eyes and mouth. Her eyes were still a bright, pretty green, unlike the piercing blue eyes she couldn't shake from her mind. She thought of those steel-blue eyes; they belonged to Frank Watson. He was so attractive, especially for a mature man. And he certainly was kind.

"You need help," she said to her reflection. "You haven't worn makeup in so long, do you even remember how to put it on?"

She called down to the spa and asked whether they could get her in. They said they weren't busy this early in the cruise, and to come down at her leisure.

She stood up in sudden determination. She'd get it all: hair, nails, facial, massage, body wrap, everything. It was time to splurge and feel good about herself again.

She spent the rest of the afternoon being pampered by a staff of beauticians and loved every minute of it. Her hair was cut and conditioned and she enjoyed a fragrant facial. Following a hot-rock, deep-tissue massage, she sat wrapped in a luxurious robe, so relaxed she could barely move. A smiling woman worked busily on her fingernails while another immersed her feet in some warm ooze that was supposed to make the skin instantly soft and supple. It smelled kind of funny, but she didn't care; it felt wonderful. From her recliner she could see out one of the windows in the spa. The sun was setting.

"Good night, Tom," she whispered. Tears of farewell filled her eyes and a warm calmness suddenly surged through her, as if he was answering her. She let out a heartfelt chuckle.

"You have big date tonight?" The manicurist giggled.

"Oh, no. Not at all."

"Is shame. You so beautiful."

Debra blushed. She smiled at the girl and thanked her. She hadn't heard that compliment for quite a while. Tom used to tell her that often.

"You go out looking, then?" the girl laughed.

Debra joined her. "Yes. Maybe I will go out looking for a date tonight."

There was a long pause as she thought about what to do this evening. She didn't gamble, so the casino was out. She thought she'd like to go dancing but didn't want to go alone. She sighed.

"I think I'll have a nice dinner in the dining room and then go to that music show tonight. Then I think I'll turn in after that. I haven't slept very well lately."

"Well. You be best-looking there." The manicurist began to laugh again.

Debra smiled wryly. *Yeah, best-looking. So what?* she thought. *Who's going to notice a dolled-up old bag like me?*

Debra arrived at the theater shortly before they opened the doors. A line had already formed waiting to get in. She stood against the wall out of the way and waited, looking around for her brother and sister-in-law. Suddenly the doors opened, and people surged forward, pushing their way in to scramble for the best seats. She waited, knowing plenty of good seats would be available. After the initial rush, she walked in and selected a middle seat in a middle row. With twenty minutes before the show would start, she asked the waiter for a bottle of water and a glass of red wine and sat back to relax.

"Deb! Hey, Deb!" came a familiar voice. She looked up and saw Paul and Becky making their way down the row to join her. She smiled, so happy not to be alone.

Over the next twenty minutes, people filed into the theater occupying most every seat. Eventually all the seats in her row filled up except the one to her right. She was grateful for having some elbow room. Right before the lights were lowered a man pushed his way through the people in her row to the empty seat next to her.

"I sure am glad you saved me a seat," Dave said as he plopped down.

She smiled at him. "I wasn't saving the seat, but you certainly are welcome to it." He still wore that same cheesy outfit he'd had on at breakfast, but now it was wrinkled and stained. Obviously he had been drinking throughout the day. She wasn't too put off by it, though. She was happy to have the company of a friendly face. She introduced Dave to her brother and his wife.

Becky smiled. "It's so nice to meet you, Dave." Paul, on the other hand, gave Dave a rather cool welcome and shot his sister one of those big-brother "You-gotta-be-kiddingme" looks. Debra grinned sheepishly and sat back to enjoy the show as the lights dimmed and the orchestra started playing.

During the show, Dave was polite and amusing. He sang along with some of the songs in a terrible off-key voice, knowing only some of the words. It was all Debra could do to keep from giggling. She was very conscious of her bare right arm and hand on the armrest between them. About halfway through the show, Dave lightly placed his hand on hers. At first it was flattering and a bit thrilling; it had been a long time since a man held her hand. But after a few minutes there was something… something a little creepy about it. Was it the fact that a man other than Tom was touching her? Or was it just that Dave was touching her? Gently she pulled her hand out from under his.

"You okay?" he asked.

"Sure. But we just met, didn't we?"

"Oh. Right. Sorry." They sat in silence for the rest of the show.

At the final curtain, the four of them stood up. Since they were seated in the middle of the row they had to wait for their row to clear out before exiting. Dave and the two women chatted about the music, which brought back a lot of fond memories. Paul stood silently and kept an eye on the new guy.

"So, what did ya think of the show?" Dave asked.

"Wonderful. Such talented performers! Made me feel young again," Becky cried.

"How about you, Dave? What did you think?"

"Oh, I liked it. I like that music. Not so good memories, though."

Debra looked at him, curious but unwilling to pry.

"I had a rough childhood in LA," he continued. "No big deal. I overcame it. And look at me now." He spread his arms wide and began to laugh, teetering a bit drunkenly. She took his arm to steady him.

"Can't keep your hands off me, can ya, sweetheart?" He snickered. "What say you and me go somewhere and have a few drinks? Night's still young. Whattaya say?"

Paul moved between them. "She's actually with us tonight. Maybe some other time."

Dave stared back at him and smiled a devilish sneer. "Sure, sure. No problem. Didn't mean to intrude. Like you said, some other time."

Although Debra was proud of her brother and the gallant way he stood up for her, this time she shot a look at Paul for butting into her business. By this time most of the people in their row had left, so she pushed Dave along toward the exit.

"First of all, Dave, I'd say you've had quite enough to drink already. And secondly, I'm exhausted and I think I'm going back to my cabin and go to bed."

"Alone?"

"Yes, Dave. Alone. I've gotten used to sleeping alone since my husband died and I quite enjoy it." It was a lie, but she didn't want to give Dave any ideas. The truth was she was lonely and some nights she yearned for the tender company of a man. And, to be honest, the thought of sleeping with Dave was appealing. But she wasn't going to let him know that. At least, not yet.

"Well, if you change your mind, honey, I'm your guy. I mean I never got any complaints, if ya know what I mean."

"I'm sure I do. Believe me, if I change my mind you'll be the first I call."

The murmur of the crowd noise was suddenly split by a shrill voice. "Hey, Dave! Davey! Hey, Dave, over here."

Dave's eyes lit up when he spotted a buxom bleached blonde waving at him.

"Rhonda!" He waved at her and hurried away from Debra's party to the aisle. He caught up with this Rhonda woman and slipped his arm around her waist. She leaned against him and they walked out of the theater together, laughing loudly. Dave started singing again.

Debra froze for a second. An emptiness filled her. *Not even a goodbye?* She was hurt, deserted, dumped. Jealous, angry, embarrassed... but mostly foolish. *What's the matter with me? So he chose that woman over me?* She hung her head. *What am I thinking? It's not like we were on a date or anything. Maybe I should have had a drink with him.*

"Never mind that jerk, Debs." Paul caught her arm and guided her to the exit, Becky clucking indignantly behind them.

Her face hot, Debra glanced nervously around the room. Frank Watson was on the other side of the theater slowly following the crowd up the aisle to the exit. She didn't understand the warmth of excitement that suddenly rushed through her body. She wanted to wave at him and say hello but didn't want to make a scene, especially in front of her big brother and protector.

Frank never looked in their direction. Debra, Paul, and Becky walked up the aisle toward the exit. The two aisles were funneling passengers into the same exit door. Maybe she'd see him there.

AFTER THE SHOW

Frank slowly walked into the theater only minutes before the show started. By this time the theater was near capacity. One of the ushers showed him to a single open seat along the side. He was surprised at the number of people in the theater, people of all ages, coming to hear old music from his youth. Did they really like this music or were they like him, there just to pass the time?

The show ran for an hour and a half without an intermission. Frank, not expecting to enjoy it, found himself tapping his feet and singing along… under his breath, of course. Some patrons got up and danced in the aisles. He liked dancing, but certainly not here and not without a partner.

When the lights came on at the end of the show, Frank was surprisingly relaxed and smiling. Much better entertainment than he expected. As everyone began filing out of their seats and toward the only exit, the crowd became instantly backed-up down the aisles. Frank wanted to make mooing sounds; the thoughts of cattle moving through corral gates again flashed in his mind. As he waited in the press before the exit doors, he glanced around the auditorium. He caught a glimpse of an auburn-haired woman in a blue dress passing through the exit doors on the other side. *Was that Debra?* He didn't get a good look. His heart began to race. He wanted to push through this crowd and try and catch her… if it really was her.

The minutes felt like hours until he made it out the theater exit and into the hallway of the ship. He began looking around, searching for the lady in the blue dress and praying it would be Debra. He moved out of the throngs of people and stood against the wall, inspecting every woman who passed by. His heart was still racing, and he began to tremble a little from nervousness. He felt like a teenager on his first date, reliving that awkward uncoordinated fear of doing or saying the wrong thing. Eventually, the theater emptied. He heaved a long sigh. He didn't see her anywhere. He must have missed her. He started walking down the hallway, depressed that he didn't get to see her.

As he passed the restrooms, Debra came out of the ladies' room and almost bumped into him. They stopped and registered an initial surprise and then stared at each other for a moment. *Those eyes*, she thought. *They're hypnotic.*

"Why, hello," Frank stammered. He laughed.

"Hello," Debra replied with a smile.

An awkward pause. He was still staring, mesmerized by her beauty.

"Um… you were in the theater, I take it?"

"Yes. Yes, I was." She paused. "I was there with my brother and his wife. They… they, uh, were pretty tired so, so they… headed back to their cabin." She paused again, searching for something to say. "I take it you were in the theater, too?"

"Yeah. What'd you think of it?"

"Oh, it was good. I really like that music. Some of those songs I hadn't heard in thirty years." She chuckled. "Brought back a lot of memories."

"Yeah, me too," hek said. "Some of those songs took me back to when I was in the service." Not wanting to be caught staring, he forced his eyes away from her.

The two began to walk down the hallway back toward the main part of the ship. The small talk was coming a little more easily, but it was still awkward. He wanted so much to touch her, to hold her hand, to put his arm around her, anything. He was being careful not to overstep her grieving.

They walked past the area where the restaurants were all contained.

"Are you hungry, Debra?"

46

"Oh, no. I ate before I went to the theater." She paused. "But if you are, don't let me stop you."

"No, no. I'm fine. I ate before I got here as well."

They walked a little farther and came to an Irish-themed restaurant-bar. Frank stopped. "I wouldn't mind having a drink before bed, though. Would you care to join me for a nightcap?"

"Oh no, I couldn't," was her initial, automatic response. *Why did I say that?* She saw the disappointment cloud his handsome face as he looked away. "Well, maybe I could have just one." She smiled.

Frank's face lit up with a wide grin. He offered his arm and she hooked her wrist lightly around it. They entered the bar and took a booth just big enough for two. He ordered a cocktail and she asked for a glass of red wine.

"So, Debra --"

"Well, Frank --"

They stopped and laughed and sipped their drinks.

"After you --"

"You were about to say --"

They laughed again and the tension vanished.

"Your brother, huh?"

"Yeah. Paul is retired and he and his wife, Becky, really enjoy cruises. They go on two or three a year. Since Tom died they've been after me to get out and join them on their cruises. I've always turned them down."

"Why? Why didn't you join them?"

"I often asked myself that same question. Partly because of the money: Tom's treatments took all our savings. But mostly I didn't want to be the third wheel."

"Believe me. I know exactly what you mean." Frank paused. "I was just wondering how you've been getting on since... Well, since -- "

"Since becoming a widow, you mean?"

He flushed red. "I don't mean to pry --"

"Sorry, I was just teasing you. I'm getting used to that word, although it took some doing. *Widow.* Somehow you just don't apply it to yourself, even when it happens. Everyone else can be widows, but it seems strange to think of myself as one."

"Do you want to talk about it? I mean –"

"It's okay. Maybe sometime. But now tell me about yourself, Frank. What have you been doing since we saw you in Vegas?"

"Oh, Vegas. How long has that been? A few years, I guess. I left that company and started my own consulting business."

"How exciting."

"Not really, but thanks." He smiled at her. "I'm happy to say it has gone very well. I'm thinking of selling the business, maybe doing some more traveling or writing a book. My son is in the same business, and he's been helping me, so it seems right to pass it on. If he wants it."

"'Watson and Son'? Sounds great."

"Well, we'll see. Now tell me about you."

"Oh, there's not much to tell. My daughter Kim is twenty-four and just got engaged to a very nice young man. I think I wanted this cruise just to get away from wedding planning!" She took another sip. "How is your wife? Maryann, I think her name is?"

"Margaret."

"Oh, yes, Margaret. I met her briefly at the wives' luncheon while you movers and shakers were playing golf. Such a pretty woman." She stopped at the change in his expression. "Sorry, maybe I shouldn't have asked -- ?"

He signaled the bartender for another round. "Would you like another glass of wine?"

She started to refuse, then made herself relax. "Why not?"

They sat in companionable silence until their drinks came. He raised his in a mock toast. "To absent spouses." He put his glass down suddenly. "Margaret divorced me after thirty-nine years of marriage. It was just final last month. We booked this cruise about a year ago."

"Oh, Frank. I'm so sorry."

Impulsively she touched his hand as it lay on the little table between them. His skin was warm and smooth. Electrifying. She found herself wanting to feel more of him. Suddenly his fingers opened and took hers in a strong grasp. Their eyes met and the world around them vanished.

After a short eternal moment, Frank cleared his throat and released her hand. He checked his watch and was surprised how much time had elapsed. "Well, I think maybe we should call it a night. I don't think I should have had that second scotch."

"Yes, I agree. I didn't realize how late it was getting."

Frank stood and helped Debra out of her seat. She was a little wobbly from the glass of wine during the show and two afterwards.

"May I escort you to your cabin?"

She was still hesitant but heard herself accept his offer. It was late and she was a little unsteady, but she couldn't bear the thought of watching him walk away. Why was she so fascinated with this man she barely knew? Why did it feel so right to stand beside him?

Initially they were the only ones on the small elevator. Each tried not to look at the other, the sexual tension between them mounting. The elevator stopped on the very next deck where four others crammed into the tiny space, forcing Debra to crowd up against Frank. He could feel her breasts against his side. He closed his eyes and took a deep breath.

She liked being close to him. It had been a long time since she'd felt her body against a man, especially a big, healthy, attractive one like him. She looked up at him and he smiled at her. *Those eyes.* An unknown warmth surged through her. She was captured by his eyes, happily helpless. The doors opened but neither of them moved.

"Venice deck?" someone called out.

Frank looked up. "Oh, yes. Thank you." The others made way as he escorted Debra out and down the corridor to her cabin. He stood by and watched her search through her handbag trying to find her keycard. "I wanted to tell you how beautiful you look tonight."

Debra smiled and blushed. "Thank you." She thought of what the manicurist had said to her today. "I went to the body shop today and had some work done." Frank laughed with her and again they gazed at each other. She found her key and turned quickly to swipe it across the lock but slightly stumbled. He reached out and caught her with a hand on one arm and the other at her waist. This time he didn't let go. And she didn't want him to.

She turned toward him and smiled ruefully. "I don't think I should've had that last glass of wine."

Frank looked at her, drowning in her green eyes. Those lips... he wanted to kiss those lips. He wanted all of her. "Don't worry. I got you."

Debra's breaths were coming quicker. She stared into his eyes and placed her hands on his arms. They were strong. She didn't expect that from a man of his age. "I... I can see that you do." She studied his mouth, wanting to taste his lips.

Frank gently pulled her closer to him. Her mind kept saying *No, don't do this.* But she couldn't help it. It had been so long since she had been kissed. Maybe it was the wine, maybe the burning desire for this man, but she was desperate to experience that again. Frank pulled her against him. She didn't resist. He slipped his arms around her waist and up her back. Debra sighed as chills ran up her spine. She leaned in and closed her eyes.

Frank kissed her. Very gently at first, their lips barely touching. He pulled back a moment and then kissed her again, harder this time. Debra put her arms around him and returned the kiss. Her lips parted ever so slightly, and their tongues briefly touched. All resistance escaped her body. He felt her soften in his arms. He slowly pulled away from the kiss and stared into her eyes. He wanted her, all of her. But he didn't want to appear too aggressive.

"I'm sorry. That was too forward." He took a deep breath and released her.

She gazed at him searchingly, then relaxed and smiled. *How gallant of him.* "No, Frank, no. It's all right. I had a wonderful evening with you. I really enjoyed it." She touched his arm. "And I really enjoyed the kiss. It wasn't too forward at all. Thank you."

"Thank me? For what?"

"For making me feel like a woman again." She swiped her keycard and the latch clicked. She opened the door, leaned toward him and kissed him on the cheek. She wanted more but was cautious not to appear easy. "It was a wonderful evening. And you're a marvelous kisser. Good night, Frank. Thanks again."

He stepped forward and put his hand against the door, holding it open. She leaned back against the door and rested her hand on his arm. Should she invite him in? She wanted to. Frank stepped close to her and she accepted one more quick kiss on her lips. "You are a very beautiful woman. I should be thanking you for making my evening so wonderful." He held her other hand in his. "Good night, Debra. I hope you sleep well."

She squeezed his hand and then let go of it. She liked how big and strong he was, yet so gentle. "Good night, Frank." Her mind was insisting, *Don't let him go.* She slowly closed the door after he turned and began walking down the hallway. He didn't look back. Would she have called him back if he had?

Just inside her cabin she sank down onto the floor and leaned against the wall. She listened to his faint departing footsteps, wishing he would return and knock on the door. That tingling warmth surged through her again. She remembered it now. It was the warmth of desire.

She got up wearily and walked to the bed. She picked up a pillow and held it close to her body, rocking it gently. Thoughts of Frank Watson's hands, his eyes, his strong arms, and that kiss kept rolling in her mind. *Oh, that kiss.* Her body was on fire. How was she ever going to sleep after that?

END OF DAY

Frank walked slowly back to the elevator but decided to take the stairs. It was only three flights up to the Empress Deck and his stateroom, and he needed to walk. *What an amazing woman.* His fantasy about her was shattered, the reality of kissing her much better than anything he could have dreamed up. He could still feel her gentle arms around him and taste the sweetness of her lips.

He passed a couple embracing in the corridor, oblivious to everything around them. He and his wife had never kissed like that... well, maybe early in their marriage, centuries ago. But she was not a passionate woman, and he had learned not to expect rapture in her arms. He chuckled ruefully. Wouldn't Margaret be surprised by the situation he found himself in tonight, mooning over a woman he barely knew?

And yet, there was *something*, some strong insistent connection, between them. He had felt it immediately. He had to find out whether she felt it, too.

He entered his stateroom and went outside to the railing. He looked down on her empty balcony and saw the light that spilled from her cabin. She was still awake. He pictured her lovely smiling face, her hand on his arm light but burning. Was she feeling the same desire that burned through his body? He was too excited to sleep, yet too tired to stay awake.

He bent over the railing and ran a nervous hand over his face and hair. *Debra.*

DAY-3

FIRST PORT

PORT CALL

Sometime early in the morning, while most of the passengers slept, the ship docked at the first port-of-call. Accustomed to the dull background hum of the engines, Frank noticed when they stopped. He glanced at the clock to see it was only five in the morning. A trip to the bathroom, a drink of water, and then back to bed. But it was no use, he was awake and not about to fall back asleep. He got up and stepped out onto his balcony. The sun hadn't come up yet. He stood naked in the moonlight, watching the waves push up against the shoreline. Only one thought permeated his brain: *Debra*; her touch, her kiss, the sweet scent of her perfume, and those eyes. Those beautiful, shining green eyes.

He took a deep breath and exhaled, trying to focus his brain on something else. He looked at the dock and city. He was surprised at how quiet it was in this sleepy little port town. Only a few lights could be seen in the city. He couldn't help but look down on Debra's balcony. It was empty, but light still spilled out from her cabin. Was she up early, or had she fallen asleep with the lights on? He closed his eyes and relived the kiss they shared last night. He wanted more. He couldn't understand this sudden and passionate attraction to her, but he didn't care. He was enjoying the new sensations. He felt alive and burning with desire for her. He had never felt this way about anyone – not even Margaret, and they had been married almost forty years.

He slipped on his swimsuit and sat in the lounge chair on his balcony, watching the eastern sky gradually lighten with the dawn. Debra was constantly on his mind. He wondered what her plans were for the day in port. Was she even going ashore? He had those two tickets for the river excursion this afternoon, maybe she would accompany him.

It would be delightful to spend a day with her. He couldn't wait to get off the ship and feel solid ground below his feet.

When the sun rose, Frank dressed for a day in port, took one more glance at Debra's empty balcony, and left for the dining room. He ate a leisurely breakfast, hoping to see her there. But she never showed. He thought about stopping by her cabin or calling her, but he didn't want to bother her. At least that's what he told himself. The truth was that he was a little embarrassed about the liberty he had taken last evening. He had literally just met her, then possibly ruined a nice evening by forcing a kiss on her. He didn't know how she felt about that this morning and he was afraid to find out. The last thing he wanted to do was drive her away.

It was late morning when Frank took the elevator to the lower deck that provided the only exit to shore. All along he kept searching for Debra among the exiting passengers. He followed the concrete dock into a building featuring several duty-free vendors selling just about everything, especially liquor, cosmetics, jewelry, and watches. He had no choice but to go through this building. There was no way around it and it took up the entire concrete dock. Anyone wanting to get to town had to go through this sales venue.

Frank bought a coffee and sat at a small café table inside the mall. He'd wait to see if she showed. He thought the safest way to talk to her would be to "accidently" bump into her. He had to know what she thought of him.

He sat sipping his coffee, carefully scrutinizing the passengers as they left the ship. After a while he noticed Dave Sorenson disembark and head his way. As usual, he was hard to miss. Today he wore white slacks, a brightly colored flowered Hawaiian-style shirt, large dark aviator sunglasses, and a white fedora. Frank wondered how much of this creep was real and how much was show. He sure looked the part to draw attention to himself. He watched him enter the duty-free shopping mall.

Dave stopped first at the cigar counter and perused the various cigars in the humidor. Next he wandered through the liquor store looking at the expensive bourbons and scotches. He didn't buy anything. He kept looking around at the people in the mall... primarily the women. It was as if he was waiting or looking for someone particular. After a while, he moved on and disappeared into the city.

About thirty minutes passed and Frank was on his second cup of coffee when he looked up and saw Debra leaving the ship. His heart jumped. He stood to wave foolishly at her, then froze. She was talking and laughing with a young family.

Accidentally bumping into her now was out of the question. He couldn't be around a crowd when his head was so full of her. He quickly turned away and began exploring the items in a nearby display case to keep from being seen. She passed by without even casting a glance in his direction.

He hung his head. Disappointment descended upon him like a cloak. *I guess that kiss didn't mean anything to her*, he thought -- even though she couldn't possibly have seen him hiding there. Why was he acting like a schoolboy? He watched her leave the building with that family. His plans for a chance meeting were dashed.

Angrily he considered just going back to the ship and staying in his stateroom for the rest of the voyage. But he remembered the tickets to the river excursion. *What the hell*, he thought. It would help pass the time and it might take his mind off Debra. It was almost one in the afternoon, time to catch the bus to the river. He stalked out of the mall and headed for the square to board the bus to the river. He promised himself he'd try to enjoy it... alone.

But she was so lovely. And something about her made him long to be near her again. Soon.

MORNING

Debra woke in the middle of the night, still clothed, the pillow pressed tightly against her body. She got up, undressed, and climbed back into bed. Again she pulled the pillow close to her, draping one long leg over it. Frank's kiss still lingered on her lips. She smiled. Too tired to roll over and turn out the light, she drifted back into sleep.

The morning sun burst through the sheers that covered the door to her balcony and into her eyes. She rolled away from the light, sleepily enjoying the pressure of the pillow between her knees. The memory of the kiss rolled through her brain again and suddenly she was wide awake, remembering everything they had said and done at her door last night. Her face felt hot, her hands and body ached… for Frank.

She lay quietly pondering these new sensations, recalling his face, his eyes, his lips, his hands. She remembered gazing at his hands at the Irish bar last night, wondering what they might feel like on her skin. She marveled at the strength of bone and muscle, yet the manly smoothness of his skin. Eyes closed, she felt those hands gently yet firmly exploring her body, discovering its hidden secrets, awaking its tenderness and passion. She slipped into semi-conscious arousal.

Her room phone rang.

Debra sat up suddenly, wide awake. "Frank?" she said. She picked up the receiver. "Hello?"

"Hi, Deb. It's Becky. Paul and I were wondering what your plans are today. Are you going ashore?"

"Yes. I have a ticket to the wildlife sanctuary excursion at one today. What are you two doing?"

"Oh, nothing much. We like to go into town and see the shops and some of the local sights. We used to do those excursions, but they are such a rip-off. They charge so much for those things and they deliver so little. We quit doing them."

"Well, this is the only one that interested me so it was the only one I bought. I don't have anything planned for the next ports."

"That's great, you can hang out with us, then. That'll be fun."

"Yes, it will."

"Did you have breakfast yet? Paul and I are about to go to the dining room. You want to meet us there?"

"Oh, no, thanks, Becky. I'm still in bed. You guys go ahead. I'll try and hook up with you in town later on."

"Okay. Have fun in the jungle. Bye!"

Debra smiled as she hung up the phone. It was so nice to have someone looking out for her. She lay back on the bed and immediately her thoughts returned to Frank.

But it was no use. She couldn't concentrate. She sat up in bed. *What am I doing?* She stood up and looked at her naked body in the mirror. *Look at yourself. You're a sixty-year-old widow batting your eyes at any guy that says something nice to you.* Fantasizing about love with a man she barely knew, who had probably forgotten all about a drink after the show and a meaningless kiss. She covered her face with trembling hands. *How can I face him again feeling like this... wanting him the way I do? How can I find out what he's thinking?*

She skipped her normal morning stretches – they seemed a bit too erotic at this point. She would order room service, take a shower, and disembark to this seaport. She'd go on the shore excursion and try to lose herself in the bustle of strange surroundings. She'd think... or try not to.

By late morning Debra joined a number of excited passengers disembarking for the first port day. She had been to this town with Tom a few years ago and looked forward to finding familiar sights as well as new ones. She checked her ship identification and tote bag for the tenth time, making sure she had her ticket to the wild animal excursion. She winced as the boisterous people behind her jostled her.

As the crowd streamed down the gangway Debra noticed the Tate family a little ways ahead of her. Once they were off the ship, she joined the family happily and walked with them down the dock, the children dancing excitedly around their parents' legs. Once they got through the enormous tourist trap of a shopping center, the family would probably head for the shops and restaurants in the town square. She helped the parents keep a tight watch on the three children as they clamored for everything in the bright displays, before they safely exited the building.

"Thank you, Miss Debra," Mrs. Tate said as she gathered the children.

"Please, it's just Debra. Have fun today."

"Thank you. You too."

The Tates turned off to the right toward the fountain in the main square, waving goodbye. Debra angled left, walking briskly to the wildlife sanctuary van waiting near the souvenir stands. The van was only half-full, mostly of senior citizens – *Like me,* she thought wryly. She took a single seat right behind the young driver and waited patiently while he checked his passenger list. He counted the number of passengers in the van and rechecked his list and then his watch.

"One more," he said. "We are waiting for one more person. We'll wait a few more minutes. If he doesn't show, then we'll go."

He? Debra's heart skipped a beat. Maybe the "he" would be Frank. *How wonderful it would be to share this afternoon with him.*

The driver collected the tickets from the passengers and returned to his seat. He was just about to close the door when a man jumped into the van. He flashed a big smile to everyone and apologized for being tardy. Then he noticed Debra and his smile got bigger.

"Well, hello, beautiful," Dave Sorenson said.

Debra blushed at the corny line. Maybe it was a bit sleazy coming from him, but she still liked being called beautiful. He wasn't Frank, but he was amusing.

He collapsed into the single seat directly behind her just as the van lurched away. She settled back in her seat and smiled. No, he wasn't Frank, but his was a smiling friendly face that she could share the afternoon with. Maybe the day wouldn't be so lonely after all.

The driver weaved the van in and around the traffic at a speed that made Debra uncomfortable. Instead of complaining, she sat back trying to enjoy the scenery and keeping her eyes away from the insane traffic on the road. Tom would have spoken authoritatively to the young man about his driving, but Debra just tried to imagine what animals she would see today.

"I'm surprised to see you here," Dave said quietly as he leaned forward to whisper in her ear. He almost touched her neck with his lips.

She had been lost in thought and the sensation of his breath on her neck startled her. She jumped away and looked back at him over her shoulder. "Actually, I was thinking the same thing about you. You don't strike me as a wildlife enthusiast."

"Well, honey, that's one thing I am enthusiastic about. A wild life." He sat back and laughed.

For some reason, when he called her "honey" it felt creepy, like she needed to bathe. She studied him a moment. He had an attractive face at first glance, but it wasn't the same kind of handsome as Frank's. Frank was dignified, classy, self-assured. Dave was actor-type, shallow handsome.

He looked up at her and caught her staring at him. A crooked, rather devilish smile crossed his lips. His eyes were brown and cold. Debra saw very little feeling in them. She turned away again as they entered the wild-animal park.

Throughout the sanctuary, the driver delivered a programmed speech about the park, the animals, and their care. He also answered any questions put to him. All-in-all, he was quite interesting. Surprisingly, she saw a lot of animals as the van passed by. During the trip she shared her excitement with Dave. He seemed to be enjoying it and they laughed together as they talked about what they saw.

The van made a turn to the right and stopped abruptly, surprising everyone. In the middle of the road a family of chimpanzees strolled along unaware they were blocking the road. Debra was thrilled.

"Oh, Tom! Look at the..." She stopped and looked at Dave in embarrassment.

"Who's Tom?"

"My husband. He died a while ago." She turned her eyes away. "I'm sorry I called you the wrong name. He and I took this excursion a number of years ago. And I... rather, he..."

"It's okay, Debra. It didn't bother me. I'm sorry for your loss. He must have been a good man."

Reluctantly she smiled at him. At last he had said something to her that sounded sincere. He took on a new, friendly light.

He smiled back at her and then pointed out the window. The chimps were leaving the road and heading into the surrounding trees. It was the highlight of their trip.

But it was time to head back to the port. Two and a half hours being jostled about over horrible roads was just about all she could stand. Mercifully the van left the sanctuary and was on its way back to town. On the way rain began to fall.

"Dammit!" Dave exclaimed.

"What's wrong?" Debra asked in surprise.

"It's starting to rain. Hell!" He slammed an angry fist down on the seat and stared out the window.

She saw that his face was flushed with anger. "So it's raining. So what? What's wrong with the rain?"

"Do you know what rain will do to this silk shirt?" He leaned forward closer to Debra. "It'll ruin it! That's what. Ruin it. This shirt cost me a lot of money, dammit!"

Suddenly she was afraid to be near him, shocked that he would get so angry so quickly over a shirt. She turned away from him and scooted slightly forward, praying that the van would reach the town square quickly.

"Hey, do you have a jacket or umbrella or anything I can have to cover up with?"

She shook her head.

By the time they returned to the souvenir stand in town, it was pouring down rain. As the van slowed Sorenson jumped to his feet and stepped in front of everyone, knocking her back into her seat.

"I guess I'll have to make a run for it. Some screwed-up day this turned out to be. Hey, buddy, stop the damn van already, would ya? Catch you later, babe." He leapt from the van and ran for the shopping center on the dock.

Debra sat quietly while the remaining passengers left the vehicle. She had no jacket, no umbrella, no raingear at all, just a canvas tote bag that would barely cover her head. The last to get out, she stepped down from the van looking for any cover. In no time she was soaked to the skin. Up the road near the square, she spotted a building with brightly colored awnings over the doors and windows. It was closer than the shopping center, and she would rather stand in the rain than go where Dave Sorenson would be waiting out the storm. She rushed for the protection of the multi-colored awning.

FRANK'S EXCURSION

The river excursion to view wildlife was a huge disappointment to Frank. Other than one alligator and a few birds, no wildlife was to be seen. *A big waste of time and money*. Thankfully the excursion was finished in less than two hours. He boarded a bus at the dock and before long they were back at the town square.

It began to rain softly just as he was exiting the bus. He had seen these humid, late-afternoon tropical showers before. They started as intermittent drops, then very quickly developed into a full-blown deluge. No time to make it back to the ship; he'd have to find shelter quickly. He walked briskly up the street to a white adobe building with large multi-colored awnings over every door and window. He made it just as the storm cut loose.

He stood and watched with sour amusement as people made a mad dash up the dock for the cover of the duty-free shopping center. Others scurried through the town looking for any shop or restaurant where they could get out of the rain. After a few minutes of pounding rain, he saw that he was the only one outside. He didn't mind, he liked storms and it was fairly dry under that awning. He watched a tourist van pull up and stop at a souvenir stand at the other end of the street. A familiar-looking man in white slacks and a loud flowered shirt leaped from the van and began running up the dock.

Frank let out a slight laugh. "You go, Dave."

Other passengers piled out of the van and began running for the ship. Still others saw the futility in running and realized they were going to get soaked no matter what, so they leisurely walked in the rain, laughing and kicking up the puddles of water. Everyone was heading back to the ship via the shopping center.

Everyone except one. A woman was running up the street with a tote bag over her head, heading directly for the building where he stood. As she got closer, he gasped. It was Debra. His heart began pounding and a warmth raced through his body.

She stepped under the shelter of the awning and put her back to the building, breathing hard. She was soaked. Her wet white blouse turned translucent as it clung to her skin showing everything underneath. Her shorts were soaked as well and hugged her legs, leaving little to the imagination. She shook the water off her tote bag and tried to brush the excess water off herself. She was aware of another person under the awning but didn't look to see who it was.

Frank stared at her, taking in the beauty of her skin and focusing on the plainly visible lacy white bra under her soaked blouse. He wanted to hold that body close to him.

"Hello, there. Enjoying the weather?" His voice sounded absurdly loud to him.

Debra looked up and froze, speechless. *This can't be happening*. All she could do was stare at him. Why was he there, now? After a few moments of taking in his smile and feeling mortified about her appearance, she whispered his name. It was all she could think of to say.

Frank stepped closer to her. She didn't back away. She kept looking at his face with that radiant smile. His deep blue eyes scanned her wet body. "My, my. You look so – "

She broke into a raucous laugh. "No! Don't say it. Oh, my God! I must look a mess." She plucked the wet blouse away from her skin, but it was no use.

"Actually, Debra, you just look wet. Beautiful and wet."

"Thanks, but I seriously doubt I'm beautiful right now. I feel so embarrassed for you to see me like this."

"Nonsense. Two minutes sooner and I would have been as wet as you." He took another step closer to her. "Besides, you still look beautiful, wet or not."

She looked away and smiled at the compliment as he drew near. She wasn't afraid or worried. She desperately wanted to know what he thought of her after last night's kiss. Did he want to kiss her again or forget it ever happened? She wanted a deeper, harder kiss. Her heart raced with thoughts of him touching her.

"You look cold," he said. He put his arm around her shoulders and gently pulled her close to him. She thought she should resist, but couldn't bring herself to do so. She wanted to be close to him. She wanted his arms around her. She wanted to feel that tingle that she felt last night with his kiss. Again it felt so right to be near him.

Frank brought her against him and wrapped his other arm around her waist. She melted into his body. He was right, she was cold and he was so warm. She felt safe, comfortable… and other feelings she hadn't felt in a long, long time. She placed her hands on his sides, feeling his body, and breathed in his scent.

He took a deep breath, absorbing the sensation of her body against his. Her warm breath stirred the hairs on his arm. It excited him to have her so close, especially in a see-through wet blouse. He wanted her. He wanted to caress her cheek, her breasts. He wanted to make love to her. But he still wasn't sure how she felt about him after last night's kiss. The last thing he wanted to do was be too aggressive and drive her away.

He looked down at her, soaking wet in his arms. She raised her head to him. They stared into each other's eyes and again time stopped. He leaned down and she closed her eyes as he kissed her. A strong kiss. Her arms went around his waist. *Don't pull away*, she thought. But he did. Her breath was coming in quick short spasms. She couldn't let him go this time. She had to know how he felt. She placed a hand behind his head and kissed him. It was a passionate kiss, open-mouthed, long and hot and wet.

Startled and thrilled, Frank wrapped his arms around her torso and pulled her closer to him, holding her tight. They pressed their bodies together. She let out a soft moan as her tongue explored his mouth. His manhood grew and throbbed in anticipation. His passion was coming out and he kissed her with a ferocity he had never known. He moved his hands from her back to her sides near her breasts, longing to caress them, wondering whether her nipples would harden at his touch. But he didn't want to be too aggressive. He couldn't know that she ached for him to continue, wanting to feel his hands exploring her body.

Slowly he pulled away from her passionate kiss and raised his head, breathing heavily. The rain had stopped. The sun was peeking out through broken clouds. The quick storm had run its course. People were again milling around the town, some staring at them. He chuckled.

"What's so funny?"

"There are people around. The rain stopped. I never noticed any of it. You, you are wonderful. What a great kisser." He held her tight.

Debra looked around at the people who were now watching them. She smiled and turned back to him. His smile radiated his desire for her. He didn't have to say it. She knew. She now knew that he wanted her as much as she wanted him. She nestled her head against his shoulder and chest.

"I think we should get you back to the ship and out of these wet clothes."

He cares. It had been a while since she had experienced someone caring for her. She didn't want to let go of him, afraid that she might not get him back. But she took a deep sigh and nodded agreement. He let go of her reluctantly and for a terrible moment she thought she would fall. She felt so comfortable, so safe, in his arms. She took another deep breath and looked around the town. The Tate family was walking toward her on their way back to the ship. They hadn't seen her yet. She broke away from him.

"Oh, Lord, I must look a fright."

"You look fine. What's wrong?"

Without an explanation she turned to look through some brightly colored sun hats displayed by a nearby street vendor, all the while keeping an eye on the approaching family. As they drew alongside she plunked a vivid green hat on her head and whirled to face them.

"Boo!"

Annie shrieked with delight. "It's Miss Debra!" The other two children hung back near their mother, smiling shyly. Then they were all crowding around her, talking excitedly about their day. She replaced the sun hat and gave Annie a hug. It seemed only natural to stroll back to the ship with the Tates, only natural to make an evening swim date with them, only natural to relax and enjoy herself in their midst. Only natural to leave behind this man she now knew she loved.

They walked through the town square and Debra guiltily glanced back at the white adobe building with the multi-colored awnings. Frank was gone.

They were about to enter the tourist shopping area when she noticed Paul and Becky walking a little further ahead of them. Their arms were laden with bundles and shopping bags.

"Paul!" Debra cried. She turned to Mrs. Tate. "That's my brother and his wife." She shouted again and this time Paul stopped and turned around. He waved back at her and waited for her to catch up.

Debra introduced the Tates to Paul and Becky Smith. The children became restless and irritable as they chatted, so the young couple soon excused themselves and headed back to the ship.

Becky turned to her sister-in-law excitedly. "Look at this great stuff, Deb. Won't they love it?" She began showing her the trinkets and souvenirs she had bought for their kids and grandkids.

68

"Come on, Becky," Paul scolded. "You can show her all this back on the ship. I need to sit down."

"Oh, all right, you poor, tired old goat." Becky grabbed her parcels and started for the mall. Paul smiled and winked at his sister, who snickered. As they approached the mall entrance, she spied Frank standing near the entrance watching her interact with her brother and the Tates. She stopped in her tracks.

"Are you all right? You act like you'd seen a ghost," Paul said, grabbing her arm. She stared at Frank, unable to control her smiling.

"I'm fine, Paul, thanks. You guys go ahead, I'll catch up with you later and you can show me all that stuff you bought."

He followed her gaze. "You know that guy?"

She nodded. "Believe it or not, yes. He was a business associate of Tom's. We met him and his wife at a conference in Vegas years ago. He's a very nice man named Frank Watson."

"You going to be okay? I mean, I can hang around if you want."

Debra smiled. "No, thanks, big brother, you go on ahead. We bumped into each other yesterday. What a fluke we'd end up on the same cruise." She waved them on cheerfully, then looked back at the entrance to the tourist shops. Frank held the door open for her with a wide grin. She couldn't help but smile back at him.

"Sorry I walked away back there. That was stupid. I just…"

"I know. It's okay."

Arm in arm they walked through the duty-free shopping area and back to the ship without noticing anything except each other. They stood in a crowd of soaking wet people waiting for the elevator. He put his arm around her shoulder.

"Debra, have dinner with me tonight?"

"All right, Frank." Her heart lifted in sudden happiness.

He smiled and sighed as if he had been holding it in for a long time. "Do you like Italian?"

The elevator doors opened and the throng of people crammed in, calling out floor numbers to the person standing by the control panel. He pulled her close. Once again they were forced together by the mass of humanity squeezing into this elevator. Debra stood in front of him, her back to him. When Frank put his hands around her waist she leaned back against him, achingly aware of him. As he was of her.

The elevator bell dinged and the doors slid open. He looked up at the numbers; this was her deck. He quickly released her and followed her out of the elevator. Outside they stared at each other for a moment and then broke into laughter like a couple of teenagers who had just gotten away with fondling each other in a public place.

"You need any help changing your clothes?" he asked with a smile.

"I think I can manage, Mr. Watson. Thank you very much."

"As you wish, my lady." He walked her toward her cabin and stopped at the foot of the staircase that led to his stateroom.

"Last chance. I'm really a good helper when it comes to changing clothes."

"Yeah, I bet you are," she snickered.

"Okay. Then meet me at the Italian restaurant tonight at seven."

She nodded and took a couple of steps away. She stopped suddenly. She returned and gave Frank a very tender hug and a kiss on his cheek. "I'll see you at seven." She walked off to her cabin.

Frank returned to his stateroom. He took a long hot shower and lay on the bed remembering the passionate kiss they had shared in the rain. The attraction to her was powerful. He turned over, the passion in him building. He wasn't sure he could wait for tonight.

ITALIAN DINNER

"So. Debra Dawson, on the same cruise with me. What a coincidence."

He poured her a glass of red wine, its color nearly matching the reflection of the candlelight in her hair. It was a perfect evening in the specialty restaurant where he'd managed to book a table. Candles, wine, salads and pasta, unobtrusive service … so romantic. He hoped it wasn't too romantic – *Is there such a thing?* -- unable to shake the fear of scaring her away. He tried not to stare at her lovely face.

"Yes, Debra Smith Dawson. Congratulations on remembering the most boring name in America."

"It's not. It's a beautiful name. It fits with your beautiful smile." He blushed as the warmth surged through him again. He turned away. The heat from his flush didn't dissipate.

Her eyes slid to the side as she lowered her head in happy embarrassment. "Thank you, Mr. Watson. That's nice of you."

"Hey, what happened to Frank"?

"Okay, Frank it is. Cheers!"

They toasted and drank the delicious wine. There was a pause.

"I hope you appreciate what I had to go through to have dinner with you tonight." She smiled.

He looked at her, puzzled.

"I had to sit through a couple of hours of my sister-in-law showing me all the silly souvenirs she bought, and telling me who they were all going to, and why."

"You poor dear. I feel honored. You deserve more wine."

"I believe you're right."

They both chuckled. Then there was another brief silence.

"Listen, Debra, I have to say something. I'm very sorry to hear about Tom. I'm afraid I've been a bit insensitive. I didn't know him all that well, but I could tell he was a fine gentleman. I truly am sorry. It must be difficult for you. If you'd like to talk about it ..."

Strangely, she did. It was comforting that Frank had met and liked her husband and could relate to her thoughts and memories. Slowly she shared the excited plans they'd made for their future after retirement, then the devastating news of his cancer, the long enervating months of caregiving when she'd felt her own life draining away, even the relief she'd felt when he was finally free of pain. And the happy final pangs of flinging his ashes into the wind this morning. Things she had never shared with anyone, not even Kim and Paul.

Through it all Frank sat and listened attentively, rarely speaking except in commiseration and encouragement. She fell silent eventually and he took her hand.

The conversation lightened and gradually modulated to where he began to discuss his situation. Usually a man who kept his feelings close to his heart, Frank was very comfortable talking with Debra. He felt as if he could discuss anything with her. She seemed genuinely interested and non-judgmental. He spoke of the happier years of his marriage and just briefly mentioned the divorce.

Topics shifted and for two hours they talked about everything: jobs, childhood and family, hobbies, schools, world events, people they knew, and anything else that came to mind. Both were pleasantly surprised at how many levels they connected on.

Debra was in the middle of an amusing anecdote about her parents when she became aware of an unusual sensation. It wasn't just relaxed happiness; it was the pleasure of knowing that this other person was sincerely interested in what she thought. She was at ease with him, free to say anything that came up in conversation, free to respond to what he was saying -- yet so aware of him as a man, throughout her mind and body.

To Frank, it could have lasted ten minutes or ten years. He was lost in her charm and time seemed to stop. She was so easy to talk with, and so interesting to listen to. So lovely to look at. He felt comfortable yet stimulated in her company. They hardly noticed when the ship eased out of the harbor and was underway to the next port of call.

"How about another toast?"

She raised her glass obediently.

"To the City of Colored Awnings."

Their eyes met and they both blushed in the thrilling silence. They drank together and set their glasses down, filled with quiet happiness.

He took her hand again, toying with her fingers. "I saw the most beautiful sunset from my balcony tonight."

"Wasn't it lovely? I enjoyed it from the tiny balcony of my tiny cabin." They both grinned. "As you know, I'm on the Venice Deck. Where is your cabin?"

"Oh, I have a stateroom --"

"Wow, a stateroom. I'm impressed. How do you like it? I bet it's beautiful and roomy inside."

"I guess it is pretty nice. Would you like to see it? I mean – I can give you a tour whenever you want."

She paused and then replied lightly, "I'd love to see it. I'm really curious about how the other half lives."

Frank spluttered into his drink. "I'm far from the other half. I paid quite a bit for this upgrade. It was supposed to be something special for our anniversary."

She squeezed his hand gently. "It's still special, Frank. Happy anniversary anyway."

"Uh, no, we never made it that far. The divorce was final last month, but I decided to come anyway."

Debra glanced at his face. "Big changes for both of us on this trip, I guess." She paused and looked into his eyes. "I'm really glad you decided to take this trip."

He smiled back and waited for her to continue, but she was suddenly quiet. No doubt she was still grieving for her husband, and still adjusting to widowhood. Maybe she might be available. But not necessarily ready ... or even interested. Still concerned that he was being too pushy, he let go of her hand without noticing her disappointment.

"Would you like anything else? Coffee? Dessert?"

She stirred herself. "Oh, no, thank you. Everything was delicious."

Again they were mesmerized by each other's eyes.

Frank cleared his throat and called for the waiter. Debra followed his change of mood, agreeing silently that it was all becoming a bit too intense.

He signed for the check and offered her his hand. "In that case, my dear, the dance floor awaits!"

A NIGHT OF DANCING

Debra accepted his hand and stood up beside him. "All right, but I must warn you that I have three left feet. You must be very patient – and guard your toes."

"As if *your* stepping on them would hurt."

"After that enormous dinner, it will!"

"Let's find out."

Gently he turned her about and pulled her into his arms. They tried a few simple moves to the music of the restaurant's accordion and violin. She made a false step in her new high heels and he hopped about in mock agony. Laughing, they left the restaurant and strolled upstairs toward the row of nightclubs.

The noise from the ship's disco reached them well before they got to the top of the nearest staircase. Glancing ruefully at each other, they walked gingerly into the cacophony and were swept up by the enthusiastic – and none too talented – dancers. She suppressed a joyous laugh when she recognized the two elderly men from the dining room dancing happily together in one corner.

As she jerked and bumped her way through the second ear-shattering song, she happened to look around the room at the various clientele. There, at the bar, stood Dave Sorenson. He had evidently been watching her and grinned broadly when their eyes met, raising his glass in a mocking toast. She returned his smile politely and looked back at her date. Dave was good-looking, but he couldn't compare to Frank's handsome face and features.

Sorenson set his drink on the bar and started toward her, never taking his eyes off her. She was intrigued and a little flattered that he was coming over to her, but wary after his behavior in town. Was he going to try to cut in on her, ignoring Frank? Nervously she watched him. She didn't want any confrontation… especially with Frank.

"Had enough yet, Frank? I really would like to leave."

"More than enough! Let's get out of here!"

They pushed their way through the crowd and leaned against the corridor walls while they caught their breath. He was smiling to the point of laughter but became serious when he noticed she was looking back into the disco with a set expression.

"What's the matter? Is something wrong?"

Suddenly aware of her change in attitude, she let out a giggle and forced a smile. "I'm fine. Really. I guess the noise and the dancing started to get to me. Or maybe it was the wine."

"Well, then, maybe we should call it a night. I can take you back to your cabin."

Debra laughed and stepped closer to him, playfully poking her finger in Frank's chest. "Oh, no, you don't, mister. You offered me a night of dancing and I plan to see that you keep your promise."

He smiled. "You sure?"

"Absolutely. I just needed to catch my breath and rest a minute."

"Okay, on to the next one. If you're up to it."

"Lead on, Macduff."

He took her arm and led her down the corridor. She glanced back and saw Dave leaning against the door watching her walk away. He smiled at her and nodded. She turned away, suddenly feeling dirty.

The next venue was a country line dance. Debra was amazed by how well Frank moved, how quickly he picked up the steps. Doing her best to stay with him, she found herself relaxing and enjoying the intricate routines. He flashed her a grin as he completed a tricky combination and was rewarded by her laughing applause. They sat for a moment and enjoyed a cup of coffee, holding hands and swaying together to the beat of the country DJ.

A nice-looking couple asked to join their table. While she made small talk with the woman and he conversed with the man, Debra had an opportunity to gaze at Frank unobserved. His face was so strong, so attractive, especially when he talked and laughed with animation. He had seemed so sad that first day of the cruise. She wanted to stroke his cheek and kiss his neck, and blushed scarlet when he suddenly turned back to her and caught her staring.

"What is it?"

"Nothing," she stammered.

He considered this for a moment, then took her hand. "Ready for one more?"

"With you? Yes."

He kissed her hand – just as he had in Vegas, but with slightly more pressure – and raised her to her feet. Nodding to their new friends, she didn't notice the tear of happiness in his eye.

They danced another set before deciding they were both ready for something a little more sedate.

"Let's have a nice middle-aged stroll up on deck."

"I thought you'd never ask!"

Soon they were up on the moonlit top deck, slowly waltzing to a delightful string quartet in the sweet fresh air. Soft pink lights were strung above them, turning the sedate couples on the dance floor into rosy angelic beings. A smiling chef and two servers in crisp white uniforms stood ready behind a long table covered in snowy linen, fresh flowers, aromatic coffee, and luscious desserts.

Debra floated through space, securely held in the arms of the most wonderful man she had ever known. Maybe it was the wine, maybe the moonlight, but everything was perfect. Their bodies glided together as one, effortlessly revolving to the music. She let her head rest on his shoulder and felt his arm tighten around her.

"I'm so happy, Frank."

"Me, too, sweetie. You are a delight to dance with."

"So are you. It's all so… perfect."

He held her closer and pressed his cheek against her hair.

The waltz went on and on, but still ended too soon. They joined the applause for the musicians, who were stopping for a break, and then strolled to the rail. The silvery moonlight on the waves was so beautiful, so romantic. The clear air was intoxicating. They stood there, breathing deeply, his arm around her waist and their shoulder and hips touching.

"Debra –"

"Yes."

"I want to tell you… that something is happening here. To me, at least – I don't know how you feel, but…" He took a deep, quiet breath. "But being with you is the most wonderful thing I've ever known."

"Yes, Frank."

"I didn't want to come on this cruise. Alone, that is. I made up my mind I would hate it. I mean, I hate crowds anyway, but this was a special kind of torture right after my…"

"Your divorce," she murmured.

"Yes. I was hoping my son Nate would go with me, but someone had to stay and run our business. He insisted I go."

"Unlike my daughter."

They were quiet a moment. Then he turned her toward him and put both arms around her.

"And then I saw you. At the embarkation check-in, as we were boarding. You looked vaguely familiar, but right before that I thought you were the most beautiful woman I'd ever seen." He lightly kissed her upturned face. "It gave me hope that my life wasn't over, that someday I could be attracted to someone again. I could be happy again. And getting to know you these past couple of days... I know it seems sudden, but I feel like we've known each other a long time. Would you mind if I kissed you?"

Her arms went around his waist and she rose on her tiptoes. "I've been hoping you would."

It was lovely, that kiss, the sweetest she had ever known. They held each other for a long time, gazing out to sea, suspended in marvelous happiness.

When the air grew chilly, Debra shivered and snuggled a little closer to Frank. "I believe that you owe me a private tour of your stateroom."

He smiled at her. Arm-in-arm, they left the top deck and walked on in suspenseful silence to his stateroom, not daring to look at each other. *What is she thinking? Will he kiss me again?* He opened the door and held it open for her to enter.

She stepped in and looked all around in a slow head turn. "This is fantastic!" Unconsciously she kicked off her shoes and set them by the door, as if she had been doing it all her life. Her bare feet excited him, but then again everything about her was exciting.

She wandered through the stateroom, making little comments about the furniture and décor, the relative spaciousness. Awed by the heat of desire rising in him, he just kept his eyes fixed on her. He couldn't understand why this woman generated so much passion in him. It was a feeling he had only read about or seen in movies, and he hadn't believed it was real. But here he stood, filled with a burning desire for this woman he barely knew – yet knew so well already.

"May I, Frank?" Without waiting for permission she stepped out onto the balcony. The cool wind tossed her hair about as she leaned over the balcony railing to look below.

He stared at her perfect figure; every cell in his body wanted to grab her and pull her close to him. Was she enticing him? The fantasies began immediately. He pictured himself holding her close, kissing her, caressing her, loving her. He wanted her with this sudden incomprehensible passion. Joining her on the balcony, he stood close to her, hoping she would brush up against him as she had earlier. It would be so reassuring if she would make the first move.

She spoke softly. "It's so beautiful and peaceful at sea."

He nodded in reply, thinking foolishly that her voice was like a song; he could have listened to her all night. Her hair glimmered in the moonlight.

A sharp breeze skittered across the balcony. She crossed her arms across her chest and gave a bit of a shiver.

"You cold?"

"A little."

He moved a millimeter closer and started to put his arm around her shoulders. But that might be a little too forward. The cold breeze subsided, and the radiance of the moonlight transfigured her.

"That's better." She turned her lovely smiling face up toward him. Those lips, those eyes, were too much for him to resist. He longed to lean down and kiss her. Would she return his kiss or run out of the room screaming? They stared at each other maybe a little too long, a veiled yearning in their eyes. *Am I reading her right ... or is it just wishful thinking?*

Debra waited patiently, then sighed and turned her face away. "Maybe I should go." Slowly she turned and went back across the stateroom toward the door.

"Yeah," Frank said, letting out his own sigh as he followed her. "Yeah, maybe that's a good idea."

She picked up her shoes but didn't put them on.

He smiled. "I see you like being barefoot."

She chuckled, releasing the tension between them. "Yeah, I hate wearing shoes, especially heels. I'll probably spend the rest of the trip in flip-flops." She laughed and opened the door, noting the stateroom number. "E-One-Twelve. Now that I know where you live..."

"You'll have to show me your cabin someday soon."

She paused, studying his face. "Someday, perhaps. But there isn't much to see. You can tour it in one glance." Her eyes were soft, sad, affectionate. "Well, good-night, Frank, and thanks for a wonderful evening."

Again he stood in the open doorway and watched her walk away, remote and lovely. He jammed his hands helplessly into his pockets. Halfway down the hall, she stopped and turned back toward him silently, that gentle smile still on her lips.

His heart skipped a beat. Without thinking he strode down the corridor, put his arms around her, and kissed her. He led her back to his stateroom. She didn't resist.

A few hours later, Frank awoke with a start. Something was wrong, but what? The cabin was dark but soft moonlight filtered in through the sheers. *She's gone! Debra...?*

But she still lay in his arms, where he had longed for her to be. Her body shook slightly, as if she were crying.

"Debra, darling, what is it? What's the matter? Have I upset you?"

She didn't answer him, just shook a bit harder. In consternation he sat up in bed and gently turned her face towards his. There were tears in her eyes, but he realized suddenly that they were tears of joy.

"What on earth – ?"

"I'm so sorry, Frank, I must have woken you up."

"I thought you were crying!"

"Oh, love, did you?" Now she laughed out loud, her delight so great that it was infectious. "No, I've been

82

laughing so hard about what it's like to make love in your sixties."

"Well, what's so funny?

"Oh, no, I'm not laughing at you, Frank! Don't think that for a moment. It was wonderful with you."

"Then what on earth are you talking about?"

She took a deep breath and drew him back down beside her. "It's like this, honey. All our lives, women worry about having sex: pregnancy, childbirth, STD's... all that on top of the usual questions. 'Does he really love me? Do I love him? Does he think I'm easy? Will he think I'm just out to catch him? How long can this last? Will he still love me tomorrow?' You know what I mean?"

"I suppose. But – "

"But now, in my sixties, with you, it's pure delight. I don't have to worry about pregnancy. Can you guess what a huge relief that is? There's no threat of side effects from contraceptives, no wishing the man would step up and do his part. And despite the sags and wrinkles and cellulite, I'm very comfortable in my own body... which you seem to like – "

"I sure do," he whispered, cradling her.

"– So I've been lying here in your arms, so happy, after making the most passionate love of my life..." She burst into another peal of laughter. "And all I can think about is those poor pitiful girls in their twenties and thirties, with their beautiful young bodies and perfect skin and all the cares in the world, worried about nothing except what some man thinks, some man who won't even remember them in the morning. So, of course, I had to laugh!"

He smiled and held her tight.

"Now you see what's so funny?"

"I must say, you have some interesting thoughts after lovemaking, my dear."

"I suppose I do, at that."

He sighed, caressed her cheek, and pulled the sheet up over their shoulders. "Say good night, my love."

"Good night, my love."

She snuggled close. They fell back into a sound, restful sleep, wrapped securely in each other's arms.

DAY-4

SECOND PORT

SLEEPLESS NIGHT

Debra woke again a few hours later. Soft, silvery blue moonlight washed the stateroom. The night's sea breeze wafting in through the open balcony doors felt refreshing as it glided across her body. If she listened carefully, she could hear the *thrum* of the ship's engines. *Wonder where we are.*

She rolled onto her back and looked at the man sleeping next to her. She blushed as she recalled their night of passionate lovemaking. She had never experienced such raw heated passion... not even with Tom. Frank's naked body was so well formed, so muscular, especially for a man of his age. The very sight of him lying there excited her. He was sound asleep, peaceful and contented. Her heart swelled as she lightly brushed his silver hair from his forehead. *What a wonderful man. What a lover!*

She sat on the edge of the bed and looked out at the balcony. She felt so relaxed, happy, fulfilled; so feminine and powerful. Moving carefully and quietly so as not to awaken him, she rose and stepped through the sheers onto his balcony.

The cool night air was stimulating. She couldn't stop smiling. Had she ever been outside, naked? She let out a little giggle as she looked around the ship and realized no one could see her. It was a perfectly private balcony. She stood at the rail, watching the sea churn by in the pre-dawn hours.

A sudden voice from the doorway behind her startled her. "I can't tell you how beautiful you look right now in the moonlight."

Her surprise turned to joy as she took in the sight of this man in all his naked glory. The tingling desire began once more. Crazy, but she wanted him again.

Frank stepped out onto the balcony next to her and leaned against the railing looking out at the blackness of the night's ocean. Debra turned back alongside him, their shoulders and arms touching.

"I've always been amazed at how awe-inspiring the oceans are. Enormous, with raw untamable power, and yet so peaceful and calming."

She nodded. "Tom was the same way. He loved the sea. Whenever we went on vacation, it had to involve the ocean." She paused and looked shyly at her lover. "I'm sorry. Maybe I shouldn't have brought him up…"

"Oh, no, Debra, don't apologize. It's fine. I don't mind; I like to hear about him. Feel free to talk about Tom any time you want. He was a big part of your life. You can't just turn that off."

"Thank you for understanding."

His nearness and the gently rocking motion of the ship began to affect her. She pressed her shoulder against his a little harder.

He looked at her. "Are you getting cold?"

"A little," she lied.

He stepped behind her and pulled her close to him. The skin-to-skin contact excited her. She rested her forearms on his and leaned back against him. He kissed her neck and slid his hands up her sides to her breasts. She moaned and pushed against him. He was big, even bigger than before. She leaned forward against the rail and he pressed her from behind.

There, on the balcony, in the middle of the night, they made love again. It was erotic, even more passionate than their earlier loving. She gripped the handrail so tightly she thought she'd rip right through the steel. She was trying to control her little noises and moans of pleasure, but the excitement was building. She dared not scream, outside in the middle of the night. She reached behind her for his body, desperate for the feel of his skin. He held her close, one hand on her breast and the other tightly gripping her hip. Her climax was the strongest she had ever experienced. He came again right after she did.

He released his iron grip but still held her close, panting. She held on to him for support, knowing that without his strength she would collapse to the floor. They stood in silence, breathing heavily until the passion subsided. *My God, I never knew it could be like this.*

"You are amazing, baby," he whispered.

She couldn't answer, just nodded and turned slowly to face him, still holding on to the railing. She had never experienced such intense pleasure and release. *What is it about you, Frank?*

"Let's go back inside."

She nodded weakly. He helped her back to the bed, where she collapsed, then crept in beside her and pulled the soft white sheet up to her shoulders. She put her head on his chest and one arm across his body. He held her gently as they both fell asleep, spent.

MORNING GOODBYE

The sound of the laboring engines woke Frank in the early morning. He slipped out of bed and looked out the balcony door.

The slight movement woke Debra. "What is it?"

"It's nothing, we're just coming into the next port. The current must be rough here. Sounds like he's pushing the engines pretty hard." He crawled back into bed next to her and smoothed her hair. "Can you go back to sleep?"

She stretched and smiled into his eyes. "No, I don't think I could sleep anymore." She glanced outside. "Dawn already?"

"You want me to order some breakfast for us?"

She sat up in bed and held the sheet across herself. Breakfast in his stateroom would be wonderful. But, if she stayed much longer, she might attack him again in a fit of passion. She hid her face from him, wondering what he was thinking. "Oh, no, thanks, Frank. I'd better go back to my cabin and freshen up, get ready for the day."

He watched her for a moment, then turned away to hide his disappointment. "Well, if you feel you have to. Okay if I call you later?"

She got up and breezily slipped into her dress. "I would like that." She stuffed her underwear into her purse and picked up her shoes. She walked to the door and opened it, then stopped and looked at him across the room.

They were both waiting.

He didn't move toward her. "I'll be seeing you later, then."

She returned his smile and nodded. She walked barefoot out into the hallway, letting the door close behind her. She stopped, hoping that he would open the door and call her back like he had last night. But there was no sound or movement; no door opened. Now she was scared that she might not see him again. He seemed disappointed when she left, but why didn't he say anything? Why didn't he try to convince her to stay? Maybe last night was too much for him. Maybe he didn't feel the same way about her that she felt about him. For a second she thought about going back, but decided to wait and see how this played out… after her passion settled down.

Back in her cabin, she picked up the phone and ordered some coffee and fruit. She opened her balcony door and enjoyed the light rain, contemplating the little puddles on the floor. Would it be raining all day in port? This time she'd take an umbrella. And Dave had better not be anywhere around.

The rain slowed to a drizzle and then stopped. She took a long hot shower, remembering last night. *If I hadn't lived it, I wouldn't believe it.* The whole night had been magical, extraordinary. She'd never felt anything like that before: the raw passion, the surrendering love, the thrills, the excitement... and the orgasms. She drew in a breath. *My, my, who'd've thought...?* She blushed crimson. He was such a wonderful lover. But above all, she treasured this new sense of true communication.

A knock on the door interrupted her. The coffee smelled delicious, the fruit looked ripe and enticing, and the steward was doubtless one of the nicest people on earth. "Thank you so much. Please take that to the balcony."

Wearing the ship's luxurious robe, she patted the cushions dry and poured steaming coffee into the cool shining cup. The early rain had washed the air clean. Debra savored two cups and lingered at the railing looking at the port town. Her favorite thing about cruising was waking up in a new place. The buildings and streets of this port glistened and sparkled. *How corny, but my heart and body are doing the same thing.*

She laughed at herself and caressed her cheek, remembering Frank's arms. What a passionate and tender lover he was, so concerned with pleasing her, so exciting in his touch. She blushed to think of herself in his bed, arching her body into his hands, her excitement rising and cresting. She had said things to him that people didn't ever really say to other people, even to those they loved. Only characters in books, breathless beauties and handsome bare-chested lovers in chick flicks, talked like that.

But he had said such things to her, too, and she had gloried in it. She heard his voice in her ear again, deep and intimate, telling her how beautiful she was. She wondered at her own capacity for joy, so much deeper than she had known.

What is he thinking and feeling this morning? Is this real? But... at our age?! What will it be like to see him again?

The phone rang inside her cabin. She could hardly breathe as she answered it.

"Good morning, Debra. How are you doing?" he said matter-of-factly.

"I'm fine, Frank, how about you?"

"Just fine, thanks. Hope you slept well."

She paused. He knew perfectly well how she had slept. Perhaps he regretted – or, worse, didn't even care about – last night; they had had quite a lot of wine. *Better play it cool.* "Extremely well, thank you, best sleep I've had in ages."

She thought she detected a catch in his voice. "Well, that's great, same here. Um, we talked at dinner about going into port today. Are you interested in tagging along with an old man?"

"Oh, yes," she said softly. "I would love to."

He cleared his throat. "Great. I'll be down to pick you up in twenty minutes, then."

"Thank you, Frank."

"Goodbye, then, Debra."

She replaced the receiver gently, dizzy, her heart hammering in her chest. *He wants to see me again.* She hugged herself and spun around to her tiny closet. What on earth should she wear?

The phone rang again. She answered joyously, "Yes?"

"Well, you sure seem happy this morning. Have a good rest?"

"Oh, hello, Paul. Yes, as a matter of fact, I haven't slept like that in years."

"Ocean travel must agree with you."

"Yes, that must be it." She giggled. "How was your night?"

"Hell, I can't remember the last time I had a good solid sleep. Becky snores so damn loud I'm lucky to get two hours of unbroken shuteye any night."

"As I recall, you do a bit of snoring yourself." They laughed together. "You guys going ashore?"

"I don't know. It's supposed to rain on and off all day. We've been to this town before. Not much to see or do. The shops only sell souvenir crap. We're thinking about hanging around on the ship today, maybe hit the casino or take the cooking class. If we get bored, we may take a walk into town. How about you? You going to town?"

"Yes, I am, rain or shine. I want to see it all."

"You going with that clown I met at the theater?"

"Who? Oh, Dave. For heaven's sake, no."

"Good. I didn't like that sleazeball. Something creepy about him. You going alone? I don't like you going there by yourself. I'll go with you if you want."

She smiled fondly. "Paul, you are the dearest man alive. Thank you for the offer. But I'm not going alone. I'm going with Frank Watson. You met him yesterday. He's a very nice man. A gentleman."

"Oh, yes. I remember him. Nice guy. I liked him. Well, have fun. And, hey, if he bothers you, let me know. I'll set him straight about messing with my little sister."

"You bet! Have a great day. Love you." She hung up and reflected for a moment on how lucky she was to have him. Then she went happily back to the question of utmost importance.

What should she wear to see *him* again?

GOING ASHORE

After Debra left his stateroom, Frank ordered coffee, slipped on his robe and stepped out onto his balcony. When room service arrived, he came in to pour himself a cup and then went back outside.

He was so confused. Watching her walk out this morning was one of the most horrible feelings of loss he had ever experienced. Why would he feel that way over a woman he just met a few days ago? What was so special about this lady? Maybe he was too rough with her last night. Maybe she was afraid of him. Maybe she didn't want anything more to do with him.

Why am I so taken by her? Why do I love her so much?

He stood abruptly and muttered, "Oh, my God." *Do I really love her? Can two people really fall in love that quickly?* He shook his head. *This kind of relationship only happens in fantasies, doesn't it?*

He took a shower and dressed for a day in port. He remembered the discussions they had last night at dinner about touring this town. He wondered whether she would be interested in seeing it with him. He decided to call her.

He picked up the receiver and began dialing her room number, but hung up suddenly. *What if she doesn't want to see me? She left so abruptly this morning. Maybe I should give it some time.*

He stood staring at the phone for an eternity. Finally, he decided to chance it. He had to find out whether she wanted to see him again. If this was too much, too soon, then she'd let him know. He again dialed her cabin and the voice of an angel answered. He smiled, warm inside.

They exchanged small talk before he asked her to go to town with him. She accepted and even sounded excited to go with him. He tried hard to contain his excitement. Inside he was jumping for joy, yet outside he maintained an easy composure. He told her he'd be by in twenty minutes to get her. Those were the longest twenty minutes of this cruise.

When Frank knocked on Debra's cabin door, she opened it immediately. They stood in the open door just staring and smiling at each other. He couldn't believe that he had made love to this beautiful woman all night. And here she stood in front of him, smiling. He must be in heaven.

"You look fantastic," he said, never taking his eyes off her.

She blushed. "You're so sweet. Thank you, Frank." She stepped out into the hallway. "Shall we go?"

He offered her his arm and she hooked her wrist around his elbow.

While they waited in line to disembark, Debra giggled.

"What's so funny?"

"You see that guy up ahead with the white hat and baby blue suit on?" She pointed subtly.

"Oh, yes." Frank snickered. "Dave Sorenson. I met him at breakfast a couple of days ago. Or rather he met me. Strange fella."

"That's where I met him, too. He bumped into my table and almost spilled my coffee. I've seen him just about everywhere I go. He's kinda cute. And he seems nice."

"Nice? He's a weasel. I don't know what his game is, but I'd keep my distance from him if I were you."

She looked into his eyes and chuckled. "Why, Frank Watson, do I detect a tinge of jealousy?"

He smiled back in answer.

It was late morning when they entered the sleepy little port. The few excursions that were offered here didn't interest Frank, so he hadn't purchased any. In fact, he originally wanted to skip going ashore at all. But after last night, he'd go anywhere Debra wanted to go, just to be near her.

As they strolled through the market area where local merchants displayed their wares, he couldn't help but stare at her. She stopped at almost every booth and looked over the wares, even engaging the merchants in small talk. She appeared so happy, so personable, so interesting -- and so sexy. He didn't want to admit it, but he really was falling in love with this beautiful and enchanting woman.

Children flocked around them offering flowers, gum, and trinkets for sale. The town was a poor village supported mainly from the cruise ship tourism. He smiled as she gave a coin to each child, even demanding his own change as well. They both laughed as the last child ran away with his last coin. He'd never been so giddy, especially around a woman. She brought out the kid in him.

At lunchtime, they sat at a small table at a sidewalk café featuring Mexican food. Debra said she wasn't hungry and just ordered coffee. Frank asked for an appetizer and iced tea.

"You really seemed to enjoy the children."

She giggled. "Weren't they adorable?"

He reached across the table and gently took hold of her hand. She smiled at him and squeezed his hand. He thought he could see love in her eyes. Was it real? Or was he just hoping he saw it?

"You and Tom had a child, I think, right?"

"Yes, our daughter, Kim. We both loved kids and wanted a big family, but he was traveling so much and I sometimes went along with him; there just wasn't time. We vowed that we would have more children later on." She looked away and let go of his hand.

"I'm sorry, Debra. I shouldn't have…"

"Oh, no, Frank. Don't. It's okay. Time got away from us, is all. We got older, Tom got sick, and that was it. It's okay. No regrets." Forcing a smile at him, this time it was she who reached across the table and took hold of his hands. "She's a wonderful daughter and I'm blessed to have such a good relationship with her. You would love her and I'm sure she would love you. She's getting married soon, so of course that's all we can talk about."

She sat up straight and signaled their waiter. "You know something? Suddenly I'm famished."

They enjoyed a leisurely lunch and then strolled around the old town, surveying its many deserted and dilapidated buildings. Frank was intrigued by the old Spanish-influenced architecture and wanted to see it up close.

"Look at that!" he exclaimed as he rushed ahead to an old mission. He stood on the step and read the bronze plaque attached to the wall. "This was built in eighteen-thirty-two. Look at the construction of these walls. Amazing." He disappeared inside.

Debra followed him, delighted by his child-like enthusiasm. The old church was in various stages of restoration. It was dusty and cluttered with building material and scaffolding. She stood next to him as he surveyed the interior walls and ceiling, listening carefully to his comments.

"It amazes me that they built things like this without any of our modern tools and machinery. Now just look at this –"

As he took a step he tripped over some stones on the floor and stumbled against the wall. She reached out to steady him but fell into him. He grabbed her and pulled her close to keep her from falling. Memories of their passionate lovemaking flashed through his brain as he held her. He looked at her and wanted her -- right there, right now.

Debra clutched him, trying to keep her balance. When she steadied herself, Frank was still holding her close.

She didn't let go but raised her head and gazed at him. He smiled at her. She raised her lips and closed her eyes.

He pulled her closer and kissed her with last night's fever. She tightened her embrace and kissed him back with equal passion. He leaned against the wall where he had come to rest and she tilted gently against him, her arms tight around his shoulders. He moved his hands up her back. Their tongues entwined.

A sudden noise interrupted them. She released him, stood straight up, and took a step away, pretending to ignore a few men returning to their work of restoring the church. Frank smiled at her and she let out a little giggle.

"Isn't it fun being fourteen again?"

He looked around and noticed that a few more tourists had entered the church.

"Here, follow me."

He took her hand and carefully guided her around the clutter on the floor to a side door. They walked out into a beautiful garden area enclosed by high adobe walls. The only entrances were the door in the church and a single wooden gate opposite it that had been secured by the workmen to keep people from entering… or exiting, for that matter.

The church door closed behind them and the large metal latch engaged with a loud *clank*. Her eyes widened as she quickly tried to open the door. It wouldn't budge.

She turned and stared at him in panic. "Oh, my God, Frank! We're locked out here."

He snorted. "Perfect. Alone at last."

"No. The door's locked from the inside! We can't get out!"

He took her in his arms to comfort her. "Debra, relax. It'll be fine. There's a few workers and some tourists inside. If we pound on the door, they will eventually open it." He smiled at her. "Honey, relax. Look around, isn't it beautiful here?" He put his face alongside hers and whispered in her ear. "It's private. We're all alone."

His calm words relaxed her. She looked into his deep blue eyes and then glanced around the little walled-in garden. He was right… it was beautiful.

He released his hold on her and took her hand. Silently he led her along the stone path that snaked its way through the garden. He folded his jacket and laidd it on a stone bench hidden behind tall hedges. It faced a small fountain that appeared to have been out of service for many years. He sat down and drew her to him. She snuggled up beside him and put her head on his shoulder. He placed his arm around her and held her close. They sat huddled together in silence, enjoying the peace and quiet and solitude that surrounded them.

"Are you okay with this?" he asked quietly, finally breaking the silence.

She sat up slowly and looked at him. "This garden?"

"Well, yes, but – this… I don't know, what should we call it? This… affair, maybe… You and me… together?" He gazed into her concerned face. "I mean… you just lost your husband, you have a daughter… I don't want to cause you any trouble or regrets."

Her hand caressed his cheek. "Frank. You're sweet to think of me like that, but I'm fine. My daughter is grown. She has her own life. I'm sure she'd be fine with this… as long as I'm happy." She took his hand in hers and smiled. "As far as Tom goes, he's gone. I didn't 'just lose' him, as you say. He died a year and a half ago and I'm finally getting used to that. All he ever wanted in life was my happiness. I think he'd be pleased… because you, Frank Watson, make me very happy."

His arms encircled her lovingly. She pressed her cheek against his for a moment, then found his lips with hers. The hot kiss that had abruptly ended inside the church was rekindled. She craved his touch, his passion. With her arms around his shoulders, she pulled herself closer to him. The kiss got hotter. She swung her legs over his and the hem of the sundress she was wearing fluttered down, exposing her thighs. She didn't care.

He felt the passion in her kiss and tightened his embrace, his own fire igniting again. He wanted her. He moved his hands along her body to her bra line and gasped when she pressed her bosom into his hands. He dropped a hand on her thigh. The kiss continued. Both breathed in short, hot gasps.

Frank moved his hand up Debra's bare thigh, his touch a spark that burned throughout her body. *Do it!* she moaned silently. Waiting was unbearable. He reached the top of her thigh and felt the silken lace of her panties. She arched her hips into his hand and felt she would explode as he caressed her. She couldn't wait any longer... she had to have him now. She reached down and undid the belt and zipper of his shorts, then stood to climb onto him. With both hands he pulled her panties down and helped her step out of them. She turned around and sat down on his lap. All breath left her body when he slid into her.

They made love again there in that lovely little garden... not once, but twice. It was again the most passionate and intense lovemaking either had ever experienced.

Afterwards they sat together on the stone bench, silently embracing and unaware of the passing of time.

Frank sat up straight, supporting her head as it lifted from his shoulder. "Debra. I have a very important question to ask you."

She turned and stared at him nervously. He looked so serious.

"About tonight, Debra..."

"Yes, Frank?" she answered timidly.

"Dinner?" And then he began to chuckle.

She slapped him on the shoulder. "After all that? You scared me."

"I'm sorry," he said, still laughing. He pulled her close and lightly kissed her lips. "So, what about it?"

"I'd love to. But not for a while. I'm exhausted and when we get back to the ship, I'm going to need a nap."

"I could probably use a nap, myself. Want some company?"

Yes, yes, yes! She took a deep breath and smiled at him, outwardly calm. "I would love that, Frank. But I really need some rest. I was up late last night, as you may recall. Somehow I have this feeling that if you napped with me, we wouldn't get much sleep."

He grinned with her. "You're probably right." He paused. "Okay, call me when you wake up. We'll have dinner together. Do you want to go back to that Italian place again or maybe try the seafood restaurant? I'll see what's at the theater tonight, maybe we can catch a show later."

She smiled and buried her face in his neck. "You choose. Either is all right with me. Sounds like another perfect evening."

He held her close as he glanced contentedly around the garden. The shadows that were scattered throughout the garden were now gone; it was getting dark. He looked up and saw late afternoon storm clouds gathering.

"Oh, damn! We gotta get out of here and back to the ship." He stood up, fixed his clothing, and helped her to her feet.

"What's wrong?" She followed his pointing hand to the sky. "Oh, no!"

He guided her back along the stone path to the church door and pounded on it a few times. Almost immediately the door was unlatched and swung open from the inside. They both stepped back and gasped in surprise.

"Well, well, look what we have here." Dave and that blowsy blonde smiled at them from the doorway, arm in arm.

Debra closed her eyes. "Hello, Dave."

"We saw you guys go into this church a while ago. Whatcha been doin' out here all this time?" He snickered and Rhonda giggled.

Frank didn't answer, just escorted Debra past them and back into the church.

Sorenson called to them from outside. "Hey, buddy, I thought you said you didn't have anything going with that one. I shoulda known!" Their footsteps faded away into the garden.

Debra froze for a second, then turned slowly and looked at Frank. He went cold to see the shock and anger that had replaced desire in her lovely eyes. "What's that supposed to mean?"

"What?"

"Never mind. Like he said, I should have known." She turned away and stormed out of the church.

"Debra! Wait!" He hurried after her. In the middle of the street he grabbed her arm and spun her around to face him, holding her shoulders. "Come on, honey. You know it's not like that. *I'm* not like that."

"Do I, Frank? How would I know that? It's obvious that you two were talking about me. What was I, some sort of prize? A bet? A conquest?"

"No! It's not like that."

She shook off his grasp and turned to leave, but he stopped her again. "Wait a minute..."

"What's the score, Frank? And what's next? You going to swap me out for that... that... blonde bimbo?"

Now he was angry, too. "Debra, cut it out! You know that's not it. That guy's a weasel. He saw me talking to you the other day at breakfast. He came by to ask me if I had a relationship with you. That's all. And at the time I didn't. That's the only time I ever spoke with him. That guy's looking– The only reason he's here is to party and get laid. That's not me."

She seethed in the silence, a band tightening behind her eyes. "Then why *are* you here, Frank?"

"Well, certainly not for that."

"You could have fooled me."

Her words cut him. He stood straight with a pale hurt look on his face. His pain stabbed at Debra's heart. Foolishly she wished she could take those words back.

"No, I... I'm here..." He took a deep breath, collecting his thoughts before loosening his grip on her arms. He sighed and looked away as he released her.

"I'm not really sure why I'm here. At first, I just wanted to piss off Margaret – you know, go without her on a trip meant for both of us. But as the cruise got closer, the reason seemed less important."

He gazed down at her earnestly, willing her to stay and listen.

"I guess I just wanted to see if I could go somewhere by myself. I've never really been alone before. I wanted to see if I could manage a life by myself. I really didn't expect to meet anyone on this trip. Especially someone as wonderful as you."

He stepped back a bit, longing to touch her but afraid to reach out.

"And I certainly didn't expect to fall in love with you. That has been a surprise."

Her hand went to her mouth, pressing back angry tears. She turned away from him, folding her arms across her chest.

"I'm sorry. I'm sorry you had to hear the crap that came out of that guy's mouth. He's a pig. He doesn't speak for me, Debra."

Trembling, she walked away a little before stopping. "I have to think about a few things, Frank. Maybe we should just let last night – and today – be what it was and let it go at that."

"Debra, wait. Please."

"I need some time alone. Why don't we take a little break from each other, figure out what it all means? If anything."

"Damn it, Debra – "

"Thank you for the garden. It was… I really… well, thanks, and… goodbye."

She hurried away through the town, through the market area, and back to the ship.

Frank could do nothing but watch her go. How empty he felt. Not being with her was crippling.

He was still standing outside the old church, wallowing in confusion, anger, resentment, and self-pity, when his thoughts were interrupted by Rhonda's signature cackle. She and Dave came out of the old church laughing.

Frank's anger bubbled up inside him. He strode back across the street toward them.

"Where's your gal, buddy? Walk out on ya already?" Dave asked with a smile on his face.

In a quick single motion Frank grabbed the lapels of the powder-blue jacket and shoved the man against the stone wall of the church. "You stay the hell away from me and you leave Debra alone, you jerk!"

Sorenson was no stranger to angry men. Quickly he regained his composure and pushed Frank away from him. "Or what, old man? What the hell are you going to do about it? You gonna kick my ass? You wouldn't last one minute with me. I'd bust you up."

Frank stared at him with eyes wide with anger, his smile wicked. "You really are a cocky little creep, aren't you? I'll go a round or two with you any time. Any time! Just name it." He stepped a little closer to Dave and glanced at Rhonda. "I bet he's got this giant ego to compensate for something else, don't you?"

The blonde turned her head away but couldn't entirely hide her smirk.

Frank stuck his finger in the other man's face. "You mark my words, fathead. Or you'll be swimming back to Miami."

He wheeled and marched briskly back to the ship. The gauntlet had been thrown down at Dave. If he didn't change his behavior, a showdown was inevitable at some point during this trip. The jerk would have to deal with him, just to save face with Rhonda. But now, he had something to prove.

Frank was boiling about Dave and his comments as he walked. But the farther he went, the more his thoughts returned to Debra. How could he repair their relationship? After all their rapture together, it had suddenly gone south just because she overreacted to some stupid remark from a jerk. Now he was truly angry. He hadn't done anything wrong, so why was she mad at him? She had made some assumptions that weren't true and thrown them in his face. He had to have it out with her.

The rain started again just as he was halfway back to the ship. He cursed, pulled his collar closer around his neck, and ran the rest of the way. Once back on board he took the elevator to Debra's deck and stormed down the hallway toward her cabin. But he stopped at the staircase and drummed his fingers on the banister. Maybe he should do what she had asked and give her a little time, a little space. Maybe he should take a little time to think as well; after all, they hardly knew each other.

He started up the stairs to his stateroom. Better to calm down before he talked to her. *God, I hate shore excursions.*

DEBRA'S DILEMMA

Debra sat on the edge of the bed with her elbows on her knees and her hands cupped around her face, slightly rocking back and forth. She was still angry. How could she be so stupid as to think Frank was anything other than just another guy looking to get laid? That happened all the time on these cruises. Did he and Dave have something going on? She felt used, degraded. *Easy.*

The phone rang. She stared at it for a moment, certain it was Frank calling to apologize. But she didn't want to talk to him – in fact, she wasn't in the mood to talk to anyone. It was vaguely satisfying to sit there and let the phone continue to ring. She wasn't sure who she was angriest with: herself, Frank, Dave, men in general. It finally quit ringing and a few moments later the red message light began to blink.

Curiosity got the best of her and she lay back on the bed, rolled over, and picked up the handset.

"Hi, Sis. Becky and I were just wondering if you guys made it back before the rain hit. We didn't," Paul laughed. "Anyway, we're thinking of doing some Italian tonight and thought you might want to join us. Love ya, Debs. Oh, and bring Frank if you want. I'd like to get to know him. Give me a call."

Debra hung up the phone, smiled a bit, and began to cry.

"Oh, you are an idiot," she scolded herself a few minutes later. "Making a fool of yourself with these men. At your age. What on earth would Kim say?"

Laughing ruefully, she crawled off the bed and went out onto her little balcony. The rain had stopped but the air was still heavy with moisture and electricity. Her gaze swept out across the little port until it stopped on what she suddenly realized she'd been looking for: the little mission church with the beautiful garden.

Silently she relived the scenes that had taken place there, especially her last conversation with Frank. She remembered her own bitter words, and his stern, angry face hiding the hurt. She closed her eyes and heard again his kind, deep voice: "And I certainly didn't expect to fall in love with you. That has been a surprise."

Inside her cabin the phone rang again. *Frank*. She whirled to answer it, but it suddenly stopped. In disappointment she leaned against the railing and cast up her eyes in exasperation and mock despair. A movement above and to her right caught her attention. There he was on his own balcony, only a couple decks higher. She shrank against the balcony wall, but he hadn't noticed her. She watched him longingly. He too seemed to be searching for the little church in town. She stared at his face, trying to read all the emotions there. She was afraid he would still be angry -- but there was only sadness in his expression, resignation in his deep blue eyes.

Hope sprang up in her heart, and she slipped silently back into her cabin. She quickly cleaned up, dressed, and left her cabin on a mission.

Twenty minutes later she knocked nervously on his stateroom door. It seemed like forever, but at last he stood in the doorway looking at her in surprise. She held out a single yellow rose to him.

FRANK'S DILEMMA

Frank swung open the door to his stateroom so hard it slammed into the wall before swinging back and closing. "Damn it!" He picked up the phone but then quickly put it back down. She wanted to be alone, so he would let her be alone.

He was so angry. He couldn't pinpoint whom he was angry with, he was just mad at the whole situation. *That damn Dave and his big mouth. And then Debra... going off the deep end for no reason. I didn't do anything. And when I tried to tell her, she basically threw me in the same basket as that Dave. She wouldn't even listen or give me a chance to explain. What is it with women?*

He kicked off his shoes and stripped off his rain-soaked shirt and shorts. He caught sight of himself in the mirror. His body was white in its nakedness, his face blood-red from anger. He stopped short and began to laugh. *You'd better settle down, man. Your blood pressure will go through the roof.*

Frank slipped on his robe and sat on the bed, allowing himself to let the anger go. He started to think a little more clearly and began to review this afternoon's happenings. He smiled at their antics in the church garden. He couldn't remember the last time he had made love outdoors; in fact, he couldn't remember ever doing it outside. Margaret would never be that adventuresome. His joy quickly turned to sorrow as he thought how he might lose Debra over something as stupid as this misunderstanding. She had every right to feel the way she did. That guy made her feel that way.

The more he thought about it, the more he knew he had to talk with her and get this straightened out. He couldn't lose her, he had just found her. He had never experienced these feelings he had for her. He would do whatever it took to get her back.

He slid open the balcony doors. The rain had stopped. He inhaled the heavy humid air and stepped out onto the balcony. He looked out across the bay at the town. The church steeple rose above the rest of the building in the little town. He could see the walls surrounding the garden and a solemn mood came over him. The passion and love that had taken place inside those walls just a few hours ago was spoiled by Dave Sorenson. *That son of a bitch.*

He slapped the handrail and ran back inside his stateroom, where he quickly showered and dressed. He picked up the phone and dialed Debra's cabin. It rang twice but he hung up. No, he thought, he had to do this in person. He finished dressing. He would stop at the flower shop and buy some roses and then go by her cabin.

Before he could leave, there was a knock on his door. He froze. Who could that be? He walked to the door and stood for a moment before opening it.

There in the corridor stood Debra. He tried to hide his surprise but didn't do a very good job of it. For a few moments they stood silently staring at each other. Then she held out a single yellow rose to him. *A peace offering?* He smiled awkwardly and took a deep breath.

"I'm so sorry, Frank. I'm such an idiot. You're nothing like Dave Sorenson. I was wrong."

He stared at her a bit longer, then gently took the flower from her. Their fingers touched.

"Are you hungry? I made reservations for seven o'clock, and my brother hates to wait for Italian food."

A slow smile lit up his handsome face.

"I'm sorry, too, Debra."

"You have nothing to be sorry for, Frank. You didn't do anything wrong. I overreacted. I do that sometimes. When I care too much."

"No, Debra. You had every right to feel the way you felt. I wasn't very sensitive to that and I'm sorry."

She smiled. "I'll ask you again, dear. Are you hungry?"

"Right, I'll shut up. Let's go."

He lay the rose on his pillow. She put her hand through his arm and they headed up to the Chinese restaurant, happy again.

FAMILY DINNER

Dinner with Paul and Becky went surprisingly well. The two men fell into conversation right away, while the sisters-in-law watched them and pretended to discuss their day in port. Afterwards Becky showed uncharacteristic tact by yawning hugely and asking Paul to take her for a walk on the deck before bed. She winked at Debra as they said goodnight and the men shook hands amiably.

Frank and Debra smiled at each other and relaxed with another glass of wine, relieved to be alone.

"I like your brother. He seems like an upright guy. I like the way he looks after you."

"He sure does. I guess I'll always be the little sister. But now I like it."

"And Becky is a trip. I didn't really like her at first, but she kind of grows on you."

"I feel the same way!"

They held hands and listened to the soft music. The silence between them lengthened and became awkward.

"Do you want to talk about it?" he asked quietly.

She looked down and sighed, then turned and stared out the window at the harbor lights. Frank became apprehensive. What more was there to discuss about this afternoon? He thought all that had been resolved and they were closer than ever. These past couple of days had been the most joyful and exciting times he'd ever experienced. But maybe it really was too much for her.

"Debra. What is it? I thought everything was okay. Why do I have this feeling of impending doom?"

She turned back to him, shook her head briefly, and gave a slight smile. "It's nothing like that, Frank." She chuckled. "After all the craziness of today, I realized something. You said you loved me. And I just have to tell you… that I'm in love with you, too."

Frank froze. He felt his heart skip a beat, or maybe it stopped altogether. He wanted to say something, but absolutely nothing came to mind. He wanted to smile but couldn't find the right muscles to do that. He wanted to jump up and shout with joy and tell the world how happy he was. But he didn't. He sat there for what seemed like an eternity with a blank look on his face.

"I know. I know," Debra continued. "We've only known each other for a couple of days. It seems impossible. This… this affair. I kept telling myself this can't be real. People our age don't find this kind of love anymore. You see it in novels and movies, not real life, not real people. But you said it this afternoon, and I know in my heart that it's true. It's the real thing."

He cleared his throat and looked down at the table, still trying to find the right words from a full heart. But she spoke again before he could, faster this time.

"I didn't want to tell you, Frank. I was afraid I'd scare you away. And I was afraid you'd just think I was easy, jumping into bed with you like that. But I couldn't keep it inside anymore." She reached across the table and took hold of his hand, holding it with one of hers and lovingly stroking it with the other. "You are the kindest and most loving man I've ever met. Ever. And, oh, what a lover you are." Her eyes found his. "I have never been loved by anyone the way you make love to me."

He smiled and was about to speak when she broke in again, pulling her hands away, her words tumbling out faster and faster.

"I know this is probably a shock to you. I mean, how can someone fall in love with someone they just met a day or so ago? Believe me, I wasn't looking for anyone on this trip. It was about Tom, at least at first, you know, saying goodbye. Then I really wanted a week alone to put my life back together, to see where I wanted to go from here. I never expected to meet anyone…"

He touched her lips with his finger and smiled at her. "You're rambling, my dear."

In confusion she toyed with some crumbs on the table. She nodded. "Well. I guess I am, at that. It's just that…"

"It's all right, Deb. You're not chasing me away." In his eyes she saw all his love pouring out to her. "If anything, you just relieved my anxiety."

"Your what…?"

He nodded, smiling, his face hot and shiny. "Yep. Since I left you this afternoon, I've done nothing but wrestle with the idea that…" He paused and held her hand tighter. "…that I've fallen in love with you. I wasn't going to bring it up because I didn't know whether you felt the same about me. I was afraid of what you might think. But, it just kinda slipped out this afternoon."

They stared into each other's eyes, sharing volumes of feeling without uttering a word. It was going to be all right.

"Ready for dessert, folks?" Their server appeared out of nowhere and the spell was broken.

Frank chuckled. "No. No, I don't think there is anything else." He looked at Debra. "I have everything I need… everything I've ever wanted. And more." She blushed and watched the young man walk away. "Would you like to go to the theater tonight?"

"What are they doing?"

"Scenes from four different Broadway musicals, I forget which ones. Could be interesting."

"Why not? Sounds like fun."

"Or we could go barhopping and do some dancing again?"

"Dancing? My goodness! I am still worn out from last night's dancing and then walking all around town today."

"Very well, then. The theater it is."

Frank escorted Debra out of the dining hall and along the enclosed deck on their way to the ship's theater. They couldn't stop staring at each other and touching, a caress here, an embrace there. Sometime during dinner the ship had left port on its way to their third and final destination.

They exited the enclosed deck and strolled through the exterior pool area. It was a moonlit night and the stars were so big and bright they wanted to reach up and grab a handful. They stopped and joined a few other couples at the rail. Frank pointed out various constellations, and the North Star.

Debra folded her arms across her chest and nestled up close to him. He looked at her.

"You're cold. I'm sorry. I just love looking at the stars. They're mesmerizing." He put his arm around her and held her close. "Come on. We'll go in."

They walked to the theater with only minutes to spare before the show started. It was difficult to find two seats together, but they finally did, way off on the left side. They sat down just as the lights dimmed and the show started. During the show they held hands and interlocked arms. He put his arm around her shoulder for a while. Toward the end of the first act she dropped her hand onto his thigh. He rested his hand on hers for a while, then moved it slowly up his leg. With her pinkie she slowly and gently caressed him.

"Been thinking of you." He smiled, closed his eyes, and breathed deeply. Her touch was heaven.

"I hope so." She shivered at the thought of being in his arms again.

A crescendo of music signaled the end of the first act. She watched the performers running offstage as the house lights came up for intermission. She withdrew her hand from his thigh and looked at him sheepishly. They both laughed suddenly.

"I feel like a damn teenager. Would you like something to drink?"

"You know, Frank? I really don't care to see the second act. Besides, you look awfully tired. I think you should lie down for a while."

He gazed at her and smiled. "Maybe you're right. Maybe I should lie down, at that."

Arm in arm they strolled back to his stateroom and kicked off their shoes. He called room service and ordered champagne and a fruit-and-cheese plate. They chatted and laughed about their day in the church garden, the cruise, the next port, and so on, until the waiter arrived. Debra opened the slider and stepped out onto the balcony.

"Shall I pour?" the man asked.

Frank nodded. He added a tip to the check, signed it and thanked him. He walked to the balcony and handed her a glass of champagne. They toasted each other and their newfound love.

She gazed out at the blackness of the night. She couldn't see where the sky ended and the sea began. "You're right, Frank. The sea is so vast, so powerful."

He stood beside her and gently rubbed her back. She welcomed his touch. Gently he kissed her neck, slowly unbuttoning her dress all the way down. She let it slip off her shoulders and fall to the balcony floor. Braless, she stepped out of the crumpled dress and stood looking at him.

He took a deep breath. "You are so beautiful."

"Oh, Frank. I'm sixty years old."

"So what? You are still beautiful. You could easily pass for someone half your age."

She leaned in to undo his belt and zipper, letting his slacks drop to the balcony deck. He stepped out of them and ushered her back inside to the bed. They drank champagne, ate fruit and cheese, and made love all night long until they were both too exhausted and tipsy to continue. In the early hours of the morning, they fell asleep in each other's arms. So happy.

DAY-5

THIRD PORT

LATE MORNING

Debra woke and smiled as she saw Frank lying next her, still sound asleep. She looked outside. The sun was blazing. The engine noise had stopped, so they must have pulled into their third and final port. She lay back down and pulled the covers up to her chin. She was warm and comfortable, so contented after a night of intense, satisfying lovemaking. She turned her head and lay watching him sleep. *Amazing man.*

Her head was a little foggy from the champagne, but she did manage to glance at the clock. It was almost ten in the morning. She gasped and sat up. Always an early riser, she couldn't remember the last time she had stayed in bed so late. Her movement woke him.

"What's the matter?"

"It's ten o'clock, Frank. We've slept the whole morning away."

He pulled her to himself with a laugh. "Well, we made love the whole night. Why not sleep the whole morning?" He chuckled, and she smiled back. "So what? So we slept. We're on vacation. Is there somewhere special you have to be?"

She laughed. "No. I guess not." She lay close to him, rubbing his thigh and admiring him. "Your body is really something. How do you keep it so in shape?"

He laughed too. "I'm hardly in shape, although I'm glad you think so. I try and stay active. I hate going to a gym... seems like a lot of wasted time and energy. I do a lot of physical things. I've always been active to compensate for a lifetime of sitting behind desks. Now that I'm retired, I still stay in shape by doing yardwork, little construction projects, sports, stuff like that."

"Construction? That would involve some physical activity, I guess, like stirring paint and whistling at passing girls?"

He pretended to pout. "No, like climbing up and down ladders all day carrying tools and supplies. Holding heavy objects in place up over your head. And lots of jumping down to pick up the tools and supplies you keep dropping off the ladder!"

"I hadn't thought of that. Tom and I were going to remodel our kitchen a few years ago, but we dropped the idea when we couldn't agree on anything."

"Remodeling is a known marriage-buster."

"Well, whatever you're doing, just keep doing it. Because you look fantastic."

They cuddled in silence, loving the touch and closeness.

Suddenly, Frank sat up. "The engines stopped. Are we in port?"

Debra rolled onto her back. "So what? We're on vacation. Is there somewhere special you have to be?"

"Actually, yes, there is." He crawled on top of her and kissed her neck lightly. "I have two tickets to a shore excursion today. What are your plans?"

She felt his body on her, molded against every cell of her own. He was so sensual. She felt like she was starting to melt from her own heat. She put her arms around him and spread her legs apart slightly, just enough to feel him against her. Impossible, especially after the night they had, but she wanted him again. She imagined him inside her. But she would pretend he didn't affect her at all.

"Well, Mr. Watson, as you know, my social calendar is so full these days. I have so many invitations that I just can't decide." She kissed him and smiled. "Pray tell, what does your excursion entail?"

"How about this?"

He pressed his hips against her. She gasped and pulled him close. He began to breathe heavily and she could feel him growing.

"My excursion?"

He kissed her lips and traced both hands down her sides to cup her breasts. She arched her back, pushing herself into his hands. "My excursion... my excursion... involves a tour... of an eighteenth-century sugar plantation... and rum factory," he said in between hot breaths.

"Oh, my God," she whispered as he massaged her breasts with his thumbs. She rocked her hips against him. "Rum?" she gasped, and then couldn't stand any more foreplay. She had to have him now. "Now, Frank! Love me now!"

Again, the dizzying passion swept them up.

Debra yawned and stretched, then rolled out of bed and stumbled about gathering her clothes. She looked at Frank as he watched her. She couldn't help but smile at him. "Are you enjoying this?"

"As a matter of fact, I am." He lay in bed with his hands behind his head. "Watching a beautiful, sexy, naked woman wander about my room is very enjoyable... downright exciting." He sat up in bed and reached out for her. She backed away giggling.

"You stay away from me, Mister California God of Love. You... you sure know how to touch me." She pulled on just enough clothes to get back to her cabin decently. "If we're going to go on that tour, I need to do a lot of freshening up. And maybe rest for a little while."

"Party pooper."

She walked over to him, cupped his face in her hands, and kissed him on the forehead. She took a deep breath as she gazed into his eyes. "You are really something." She kissed him again and Frank reached out for her. She leaped up with a shout, backing away from his hands.

She stopped in the doorway and turned around to smile at him. "I'll be waiting to hear from you."

"You have two hours. Take a nap."

She blew him a kiss and waved goodbye.

Back in her cabin, she sat on the edge of the bed staring at herself in the mirror on the wall. She felt so happy, so feminine, so desirable. *But is this really happening?* She had never been loved like this in her life. She had never been this adventuresome, this randy, with a man. This was the kind of love and passion she had always wanted but thought unattainable. *At sixty years old I'm acting like a high-school girl with raging hormones.*

She shook her head. "This can't be happening," she said to the woman in the mirror. She studied herself, the lines, the age spots, the eyes, the chin. No, darn it, the chins.

"I'm an old woman." She paused. "I wonder if he sees how old I am? I wonder what he sees. I wonder if he will always see that."

She drew a long deep breath and stood up. "Well, whether this is a dream, or fantasy, or reality, I'm enjoying the hell out of it."

Humming, she went into the bathroom and started the shower. "My hair is a disaster." She began to sing softly, then more lustily.

APOLOGY

Frank lay in bed for a while after Debra left, reliving their night together. Never had he imagined he could make love to anyone like he had with her. Never such passion, such outright lust for anyone, until he met her. She brought out so much fire in him. This was the kind of love he had always wanted but had never believed really existed. He had thought a relationship like this was not meant for him... until he met her. Here was that special kind of love, staring him in the face, and he lay there doubting it.

"Idiot."

He threw the covers off and went into the bathroom to clean up. As he shaved, he stared at himself in the bathroom mirror. "Look at you. Mid-sixties. You're an old man. What are you doing acting like you're in your twenties?" Why this stage of his life? He wished he had the stamina of his twenties again, so he could love her longer and harder. She seemed pleased with his performance, though. She had also said she loved him, Several times.

He smiled. "She loves you, you old coot."

He ordered some breakfast and lounged around on the balcony watching the clouds break up. He took his time eating before he showered, dressed and picked up the tickets to his rum plantation excursion. He smiled at the thought of spending a whole day with her.

Time to get going. He opened his door just in time to see Rhonda walking by slowly, unsteadily. He looked up the hallway and there, in the doorway of a stateroom just two doors away, stood Dave Sorenson. Frank's demeanor instantly changed from happy and excited to angry and disgusted. He flashed that look at the other man and turned to walk away.

"Frank, wait a minute!" Dave shouted. He began to walk toward Frank, who kept on going.

"Come on, man. Hold up a minute. At least give me a chance to apologize."

Frank stopped, took a deep breath, turned around and waited for him to approach. He met Dave's friendly little smile blankly, his eyes cold with contempt. Sorenson's smile faded.

"Look, Frank. We obviously got off on the wrong foot here. And I know it's all my fault. I can be an ass sometimes – I know that. You have every right to be pissed. I just want to apologize for what I said yesterday to you and Debra. I didn't mean anything by it. I was just trying to make a joke. I guess it backfired and I'm sorry." He held out his hand.

Frank eyed it suspiciously. He looked at Dave's face. He seemed sincere about his apology, but something else was lurking below this act of repentance. Hesitantly he took the proffered hand.

"Don't let it happen again," he said as he glared at Dave. "And I meant what I said about staying away from Debra. She just buried her husband and is very delicate. So keep away."

"You got it. No problem. I promise I won't go near her." Dave gave Frank's hand one more vigorous shake. "How about I buy you a drink? We'll talk."

"Some other time. I'm off to a rum plantation."

"Oh yeah? Me, too! Rhonda and I are going there to sample the wares, so to speak."

Frank's heart sank. He wanted to forget the whole excursion.

"Rhonda didn't look too good a minute ago. What's wrong? Is she sick?"

Dave smiled. "She's just wore out. The love machine struck bigtime last night." He laughed and chucked Frank's shoulder. "Yeah, buddy, another willing victim of the All-

Night Love Machine. Okay, see you there." He walked away, humming tunelessly.

Frank's stomach churned as he turned and headed off to meet Debra for their tour.

He found her standing in the hallway with her brother, Paul, and his wife, Becky. When she saw him she smiled, and Frank's heart began to beat faster. Joy raced through him. She was the only thing he saw... everything else vanished from his sight and time seemed to stop. Her sweet, loving face was a watercolor of clarity in a tunnel of silent mist. It was as if they were the only two people on this ship.

The image faded. He'd never be able to tell her about this, it was just too bizarre. But he couldn't help but smile back at her, love pouring from his eyes.

"Frank! Paul and Becky decided to join us. Isn't that exciting?"

He smiled and shook Paul's hand, greeting Becky at the same time. "That's great! Glad to have your company." He turned to Debra. "You know who else is going to join our little outing?" She looked a little concerned. "Our good friend Dave Sorenson and his blonde bimbo."

"Dave and Rhonda?" she cried in dismay.

"Wait a minute," Paul said. "Ain't that the guy who sat with you in the theater a few nights back?"

"Yes, Paul. That's the guy," she replied.

"You sat with him at the theater?" Frank asked, jealousy painfully apparent in his voice.

"Not really, Frank. I sat with Paul and Becky. He sat down next to me."

Frank lowered his head. The thought of Dave anywhere near Debra angered him.

She took his hand and tried to catch his eye. "We are going to have a great time. You and me, Frank. Dave and Rhonda can go do what they do. It'll just be us. Okay?"

He took a deep breath and looked back at her. Her smile chased away his anger. He smiled back at her. "Okay. Just us."

"Well, the four of us will just have to stay close together and away from that Dave fella and his… whatever you called her," Becky said simply.

Debra nodded and wrapped her hands around Frank's arm. The four disembarked for town.

RUM PLANTATION

Twenty passengers had signed up for this excursion, a group tour scheduled to last all afternoon. It came complete with a bus ride to and from the plantation as well as their own tour guide. Dave and Rhonda managed to catch the bus at the very last minute and slouched down into the seats across the aisle from Frank and Debra.

Despite this, the bus ride turned out to be enjoyable. Debra spent the time conversing with Paul and Becky, who were seated behind her. Frank tried to enjoy the ride and the conversation, but he was sitting on the edge of his nerves waiting for Dave to make some idiotic remark. He was happy that the oaf stayed true to his word and didn't even look at Debra.

It was a pleasant day. The morning clouds gave way to a clear sky and bright sunshine. When they arrived at the plantation Frank and Debra hurried to put as many people as possible between their foursome and Dave and Rhonda.

The tour was interesting, at least to Frank. They toured the manor house that sat on the plantation, which Debra seemed to really enjoy. Her pleasure turned to shock and horror when they came upon the meager, barn-like cabins that had housed the workers and slaves. They toured the storage bins and the grinding wheel, where smiling laborers demonstrated the traditional way of extracting the sweet liquid from the sugarcane stalks. The women felt sorry for the thin donkey that was harnessed to the wheel. All day long the donkey would walk in a circle turning the grinder.

As they stood watching the grinding demonstration, Dave and Rhonda managed to move up alongside Frank and Debra.

"How cruel to keep that poor donkey tied up to that wheel all day long," Debra cried.

Rhonda snapped her chewing gum. "Well, that's its job. What'd ya think? It's just a dumb animal." She took Dave's arm firmly.

Debra was too stunned to reply. Frank slipped his arm around her shoulder and led her away from the wheel… and from Rhonda.

"Let it go, honey. Some people are just ignorant," he said calmly.

She looked into his eyes and let her anger go. "That bimbo is the only dumb animal around here."

They both laughed.

After the tour of the mansion and the grounds, the quartet walked through a brief tour of the rum distillery and bottling operation. Frank and Paul were enthralled with the entire process of turning cane syrup into rum, but Debra had lost interest and strolled along with Becky.

During the tour inside the distillery, Dave had walked next to Frank opposite Paul. Rhonda stayed back and loosely walked along with the other women, and it was all Debra could do to keep from slapping Rhonda for her donkey remark. Dave listened politely to Frank and Paul's cordial conversation about the distillery process and different liquors. Occasionally, he would chime in with some interesting tidbit. For the first time this week, Frank saw Dave in a better light. He was trying to just be one of the guys, and he was doing a decent job of it.

At the end of the tour was a handsome tasting room featuring the different types of rum produced here. Frank counted sixteen bottles lined up on the counter in order of weakest to strongest alcohol content. Some were clear, some a caramel color, some the color of dark coffee.

"Oh, yeah! Now we're talking," Dave blurted out, rushing to the counter to inspect the bottles.

Becky and Debra quickly took a seat at a table for four.

"Do you like rum?" Frank asked.

"I don't know," Debra replied. "I don't think I've ever tried it."

"I'll get a couple samples and you can take a sip of mine."

The tour guide gave a little speech about the tasting room, the various rums displayed, and the process for getting samples. Each member of the group was invited to sample three different rums. Dave and Rhonda were the first two at the counter. Frank and Paul fell in line well behind them.

When it was Frank's turn, he asked the server for samples of the weakest rum, the strongest rum, and a caramel-colored, fruit-flavored rum. Feeling vaguely brave and adventurous, he carried the tray carefully to their table.

Debra took a sip from the weakest rum and shrugged her shoulders. "It's okay, I guess. Based on this I don't think I'd order any rum drinks."

Frank smiled and finished the sample of the weakest rum. "That's not too bad." He smacked his lips. "I'm not much of a rum drinker, but that was actually pretty good. Here. This is the strongest rum made. Just take a tiny sip of it."

She coughed and made a sour face. "Okay. No. I don't like rum."

He sipped the strongest rum. "That's horrible! Tastes like lighter fluid." He coughed as the others laughed. "Wow. Man, that's strong. How can anybody drink that?"

She giggled.

He sipped the fruit-flavored rum and smiled. "Oh, here, honey. You have to try this."

Paul and Becky exchanged a glance. *Honey?*

Frank was handing Debra the small plastic cup to taste. Gingerly she took a small sip, expecting the worse. She licked her lips in surprise and then took a bigger sip.

"That's really good. Kind of syrupy." She finished the sample. "Okay. I like rum again." She laughed and they all joined her.

Dave and Rhonda sauntered over to them. "Did you all get your three free samples of rum?"

They nodded reluctantly.

"So let's get our plans together for tomorrow," Paul began, hoping this hint would turn the two away.

But Sorenson continued despite the interruption and took control of the conversation, guiding the topics from rum to his investment in a liquor operation in Kentucky, to investments in general, to money returns. He skillfully mesmerized everyone with the lure of unrealistic returns from an investment group he was running. Debra and Becky were enthralled by his rags-to-riches spiel, while Rhonda looked on proudly. Even Paul seemed interested. Frank, on the other hand, knew right away what he was trying to do but decided to keep it to himself for the moment.

Eventually the tour guide addressed their group. "Sorry, folks, time to head back to the bus. Feel free to purchase some of these delicious, duty-free rums to take home with you."

"Well, as I was saying – "

"Save it, Dave," Frank commanded. "Time to go." He took Debra's arm with a sly smile.

DINNER ON THE BEACH

After the tour the bus took everyone back to town, depositing them conveniently outside the rows of street vendors.

"Do you want to grab some dinner here in town?" Frank asked.

"No, thanks," Becky replied. "I'm tired and we're going back to the ship."

"Yeah," Paul added. "Maybe we'll see you at the buffet tonight."

Debra hugged them and the men shook hands. "Great day today."

"Paul, keep a good hold on your wallet," Frank began. "I'm not exactly sure what Dave's scheme is, but I'm pretty sure it's not for real. May not even be legal. He's just trying to get us to invest with him. Be wary."

Paul smiled and nodded. "I'm onto him."

Frank and Debra watched Dave and Rhonda catch up with them as they walked back out to the ship.

"Poor Paul," Debra remarked. "Having to listen to that maniac all the way back to the ship."

Frank chuckled. "Well, I have to admit, I do believe Dave was on his best behavior today."

"What do you think of that investment club he started?"

"It sounds pretty amazing. A little too amazing."

"Why?"

"Those numbers he was quoting were bogus. No one makes that kind of return on any investment. Trust me on this."

"Then why would he say that? Consider the source?"

"Ever hear of a Ponzi scheme?"

"I've heard the term, but I'm not sure what it is."

"It's basically a scam. He gets people to invest money with him, promising them unrealistic returns on their investment. He has to keep getting new investors to pay off his original investors, so they will give him more money. It's a never-ending cycle that keeps getting bigger. He pockets huge fees and then eventually quits investing all together. Then, one day, he disappears with all the money."

"And people fall for that? So dishonest."

"It is. It's also illegal." Frank pointed to a small café along the beach. "How about eating here?"

Debra agreed immediately, happy that he took charge and made decisions.

They ate dinner by the sea, sampling the local fare of fish, fruits, and breads. Afterwards they removed their shoes and walked along the beach for a while, enjoying the mild evening and each other's company.

Time stood still for them tonight. For so many years each had been consumed by just existing from one day to the next. Providing for spouse and family was the daily grind. They slept, ate, worked, and occasionally played. They planned for the future, which was always tomorrow... never now. There were good times in their respective lives, and there were bad times -- but that's all there ever were. That's the way they both thought life was. They did what they were supposed to do... what was expected of them. They had loved their spouses the best they could, but it was not even close to the feelings they had for each other right here, right now. This was true love, the passionate love both had always dreamed of. And it was a shock.

Debra stopped to watch the sun descend. "Let's sit."

"Here? In the sand? We don't have a towel or a blanket."

She pulled him down with her onto the golden sand still warm from the day's sun. They sat close, watching the sun inch closer to the horizon. She looked at him in the brilliant sunset. He returned her gaze.

"How did I ever get so lucky to meet you?" he asked. She smiled in answer. He kissed her lips. "Whatever I did to deserve you, I'm hoping I keep doing it."

"So do I," she exclaimed. She flung her arms around him and fell back onto the sand with him. She pressed a kiss against his lips and coaxed his mouth open with her tongue. The kiss grew hotter and more passionate. Neither cared that they were out in the open on a public beach. Their need was too strong.

Suddenly she sat upright. "Ouch! What is this under me?" She reached back and pulled from the sand an exquisite silver shell. She'd seen similar ones, white ones, speckled ones, in the port markets, but this was so unusual. It seemed both fragile and immensely strong.

In silence she stared at Frank.

"What is it, sweetie?"

"Oh, Frank! It's a silver shell. Isn't it beautiful?"

Tears filled her eyes. It was true. Tom's story of the silver shell symbolizing true, everlasting love wasn't a fable at all. It was true.

"Are you okay, honey?" He took her hand.

She could only nod in answer, her smile getting wider. Her eyes moved from Frank to the lovely shell and back again as Tom's voice raced through her mind.

"That's very pretty. Let me take a look."

She was just handing it to him when the ship's horn burst into their ears, signaling an imminent departure. "Oh, no, don't drop it!"

"Dammit!" He jumped up and helped her to her feet. "We gotta go. Ship's getting ready to sail. Take your shell and hang on. We have to hurry."

They ran back along the beach with their arms around each other's waists, panting and laughing when they reached the dock. They brushed the sand from their feet, slipped their shoes on, and made their way back to the ship with the last of the latecomers.

"That was close!"

"Igotta catch my breath."

They got off the elevator on Debra's deck. She started walking to her cabin, but Frank didn't. She stopped and turned back to him.

"Aren't you going to walk me to my cabin?"

He smiled and shook his head. "No, I don't think so." He stepped close to her and put his hands around her waist. "Too dangerous. If I walk you to your cabin, you'll invite me in, and I won't be able to say no, and we'll end up making love all night long, and ..."

Debra interrupted him with a kiss, then leaned back with a smile. "And what's the problem?"

Frank smiled. "You know, I really don't see one. Except... I have a few things to do before tomorrow. And I need to do them now."

She pulled him close to her. "What things? What's so special about tomorrow?"

He kissed her nose and stepped from her embrace. "You'll see, my love. You'll see." He chuckled and pressed the elevator call button. "Tomorrow we spend the whole day at sea. No more ports. It's also the last full day of this cruise. I'll call on you later tonight. You get some rest. You're going to need it."

The elevator doors opened. Frank stepped in and turned to look at Debra. She put her hands on her hips and looked up at him. "What are you up to?"

He just smiled and waved as the doors closed.

She turned and whistled her way down the corridor, the silver shell still clutched in her hand.

Back in her cabin she rinsed the shell in the sink and dabbed it dry. She walked out onto her balcony and carefully held the silver seashell up into the dying sunlight. It shone with a radiance all its own.

She gazed at the sun as it sank slowly into the sea. "You were right, Tom. Thank you."

She couldn't hold back the tears of pure joy.

CASINO

On the way back to his stateroom he walked through the casino. He hadn't gambled this entire trip. He'd been too occupied with Debra, a distraction he relished. *The real thing, at last. I'm the luckiest man in the world.*

The casino was crowded, but not too bad. A couple of games couldn't hurt. He played a little on the slot machines, but they were boring and not very lucrative. He tried his hand at the roulette table but never hit a single number. His luck was not very good this evening. He'd try blackjack. If his bad luck continued there, he'd quit and call it a night.

He found a blackjack table where the only two occupied chairs held a young couple on their first cruise. He slid into the chair closest to the dealer. He won a few hands, lost a few hands. He yawned and was thinking of leaving just as Rhonda and one of her girlfriends sat down at the table with him.

"Frank! Oh, I'm really glad to see you," Rhonda said with slurred speech. "Frank. This is Barbie. Barbie? Meet Frank."

"Evening, ladies. I see you've been celebrating already."

"It's a real pleasure to meet you, Frank," Barbie said. Her hair was as artificially red as Rhonda's was blonde.

"Likewise."

Rhonda turned to her friend. "See? I told you he was cute. Didn't I? Didn't I tell ya?"

Barbie, a scrawny woman in heavy makeup, giggled and leaned in to Rhonda. She tried to whisper, but she could be heard across the casino. "Yeah, you told me. He sure is a looker."

"And nice. He's really nice. A real gentleman."

Barbie chucked Rhonda on the shoulder and laughed.

Frank rose and pushed his chips to the dealer. "Cash me out, please."

"Oh no, Frank! You can't leave now. We just got here. Come on. Play a few more hands with us."

Afraid she'd make a scene if he didn't, he sank back into his chair and rejoined the game. Surprisingly, he began winning. He spent another hour playing cards and visiting with Rhonda and Barbie.

"So, where's Dave tonight?" he asked as a matter of conversation, not really caring. "You and he seem to be seeing quite a bit of each other."

"Yeah, he's a fun guy, I guess. He sure can spend his money. I like that in a man." Rhonda snorted and Barbie chimed in. "He smuggled on board one of those bottles of rum he bought today. We've been drinking it all day. Barbie here said she had to eat something, so we went to get some food. He's still in his room, I guess. He's pretty drunk."

"Unlike you two," he quipped.

"Yeah. Like us," Rhonda said with a laugh.

Frank yawned. He was thinking about leaving again when he heard Dave calling Rhonda from across the casino. He stumbled around the casino searching for her.

Frank pushed his chips to the dealer and cashed in his winnings.

"There you are, baby!" Dave shouted. He weaved his way over to the table and leaned against an empty chair. "I was waiting for you to come back. Why didn't you come back?"

"Barbie wanted to do some gambling and I thought it would be fun. So here we are."

"Well, you played enough. Let's go back to the room." He grabbed Rhonda's arm and began to pull her off her chair.

"Cut it out, Dave. I don't want to go now." She shook off his grip. "We're having fun. We're gonna play a while longer. We'll come back then."

There was a pause.

"Come on, baby, sit down here and play some cards with us."

"No! Come on back now."

Frank rose. "They said they don't want to go, Dave. Take it easy. You're making a scene."

"Why don't you mind your own damn business, Frank, ol' buddy, ol' pal?" Sorenson moved a little closer to him. "This don't concern you."

"Easy, Dave. Why don't you sit down here and play a few hands with the girls? You might enjoy it."

Dave stared at him for a moment. "The 'girls'? You better just butt out." He poked his finger into Frank's chest. "What are you doing up here, anyway? Trying to pick up my girl? Where's your hot little redhead?"

Anger was building up in Frank. He took a deep breath and began to walk away.

"What's the matter, Frankie? Debra not doing it for you anymore? Gotta horn in on my girl?"

Like lightning Frank spun around and punched Dave right in the face. The man fell to the floor and didn't move. Frank took a deep breath and immediately regretted his action... even though it felt pretty good to sock Dave's big mouth.

Rhonda jumped to her feet shouting a few expletives, and ran to her prostrate friend. She talked to him and patted his cheeks until he started to come around. A cocktail waitress brought a clean towel and some ice water to cool his forehead. An excited buzz ran around the casino.

Barbie slunk in next to Frank and gently took hold of his upper arm. "That was some punch," she said, squeezing his bicep. "I bet you're all man, aren't you?"

Frank glared at her and tossed her hand from his arm. The ship's security team arrived and escorted Dave, Frank, and the two women out of the casino and into a private room. They questioned the four of them to sort out what happened. After a while, they were satisfied. No charges were levied. Dave refused any medical treatment and left the room with Rhonda in tow. Barbie stayed behind with Frank and the security guards.

"You two traveling together?" one guard asked.

"No," Frank immediately blurted out.

"Not yet, anyway," Barbie added as she stepped next to him and ran her arm across his back and over his shoulder while pressing herself against him.

"Not ever." He stood up, shaking himself free. "Are we done here?"

"Yes, sir. You are free to go. You might want to avoid that other gentleman for the remainder of the cruise."

"That thought occurred to me, too." Frank bolted out the door.

He swore to himself that if this thing with Debra didn't work out, he would remain single for the rest of his life. If that was a sample of the available women in the dating circuit, he was signing up for celibacy.

Back in his stateroom, he showered and changed into shorts, sandals, and a casual shirt. He purchased a single yellow rose on his way to Debra's cabin and offered it to her with a flourish. "I just wanted to let you know how much I love you and how much I really, really appreciate you."

Smiling, she took the rose and sniffed it. She put a hand behind Frank's head and kissed him softly and lovingly. Then she beckoned him inside and escorted him to the balcony, where he stopped in the doorway.

While he had been making his mysterious arrangements and playing at the casino, Debra had ordered a bottle of wine and a fruit-and-cheese plate. They were set up on her balcony along with several candles. Pleasantly surprised, he smiled at her. She was so beautiful, standing there in a long, sheer black nightgown.

"What do you think?"

"This is wonderful," he said. "I wasn't expecting this at all." He stepped out onto the balcony. "You are so beautiful. You continue to amaze me."

She did a little hop and clasped her hands together. "I'm so happy. I wanted to please you." She took his arm. "I wanted you to like this. I wanted our last couple of nights to be special… just you and me. You don't mind?"

"Mind? Hell, no, I don't mind. I love this." He took her in his arms and hugged her. He didn't let go. He wanted to be frozen at that moment with that feeling of joy forever. Debra stood quietly, blissfully in his arms.

"Wine?" she finally asked.

Frank released her and nodded. "Sure. I'll have a glass." He sat in one of the two deck chairs and removed his sandals.

She poured two glasses and handed one to him, touching her glass to his. "To love…" she said and took a sip.

"To love."

She sat in the deck chair across from him. They talked, reminisced about their week, laughed, drank, and ate. She poured another glass of wine and stood before him.

"I know what you're doing," Frank said with a smile. "You're trying to get me drunk so you can take advantage of me."

She laughed. "I don't think I need to do much to take advantage of you."

"Oh. Are you saying I'm easy?"

She bent over in front of Frank, coyly revealing her breasts in her nightgown. Then she lifted his chin with her finger and kissed him… a long, wet, kiss that seemed to last for hours. It was a kiss he felt all through his body.

When their lips finally parted, he gazed at her. "Wow. I guess I am easy. You win." They both laughed. He seized her waist and pulled her down into his lap. The deck chair made an awful groan and creaked.

"Oh!" She jumped up off his lap. "I guess I'm too fat for that chair."

"You? Come on." He stood. "You are perfect, my dear. You have an amazing body that most younger women would kill for." He checked the chair for damage, but it appeared to be unscathed. "See, the chair is fine. If anything, it was my fat ass it was complaining about."

"You are gorgeous, Frank Watson. It didn't start creaking until I sat on it."

"Along with me... Hell, I was in the casino earlier and saw women twenty years your junior who would have given that chair something to complain about. You put them to shame."

She opened her mouth to ask him about the casino, but he pulled her to him and kissed her. At first she resisted, but then she melted into his embrace. Their tongues found each other, and the short hot breaths began. He pulled away slowly, letting the kiss hang on her lips.

"Look at me, Debra," he whispered.

She opened her eyes and locked onto his.

"Shall we step inside?"

She nodded slowly.

Inside, next to the bed, she unbuttoned his shirt and undid his belt and zipper. She pulled off his shirt as his shorts fell to the floor. She looked at him, smiling. "No underwear, Frank?"

He stood erect in front of her.

"Is all that for me?" She didn't wait for a response. Gazing lovingly into his eyes, she dropped slowly to her knees. Her own excitement was building.

Frank became lost in it. His hips moved uncontrollably with unaccustomed excitement. His pleasure was becoming too much for him to contain any longer.

Debra stood and gently pushed him onto her bed. She kissed his body as she slowly moved to his mouth. She lay lightly on top of him and kissed his nose and smiled.

"Now don't go away, Mister Big-Time-Stateroom-Gambler... and don't you dare move. I'll be right back." She stood and stepped into the bathroom doorway. The bedroom was dark, lit only by the moonlight seeping in through the sheers and now the soft light escaping through the bathroom door. Her figure was backlit. She let her long, black nightgown fall off her before closing the door. He heard her laugh softly as the water ran.

Moonlight flooded her cabin as she left the bathroom and approached the bed. He lay stretched out on his back, his arms resting behind his head, breathing deeply. He gasped when he saw her.

"You're so beautiful."

She crept onto the bed and knelt beside him, drinking in the sight of his long, well-formed body lying in her bed. He reached for her slowly, but she gently pushed his wrists down just above his head.

"Debra. Don't you want me to touch you?"

Her hair hung long and soft over her bare breast. She slowly shook her head and then kissed him sweetly.

"More than anything, Frank. But last night, in your room, you gave me such pleasure I had never known before. Now I want to concentrate on you."

She bent down to kiss him softly, a faint moan escaping both their throats. Each felt the magnetism of the other's body, the same pull of desire, the same sense of coming home.

And the same rising excitement.

They kissed more passionately, his hands still pinned down. Her lips left his to explore his face, his hard cheekbones and broad forehead. She rubbed her cheek against his and then kissed his ear and his neck, inhaling his male scent and touching him very lightly with the tip of her tongue. Shivers coursed through his body with every kiss. Lightly she caressed him, loving the feel of his skin, of the bone and muscle beneath. Slowly she kissed his shoulders, his chest, his belly, his sides, his ardent manhood, his hips and thighs and calves, her hair trailing across his quivering body. He arched his hips toward her, craving her touch.

She returned to his mouth and lay gently against him, hungry but reserved.

"Would you like to touch me now?"

She released his hands, laying her own on his chest. They gazed into each other's eyes for a moment, measuring thoughts and emotions, searching each other for the truth. Then, Frank's passion could no longer be withheld; he swept her into his arms and began to love her slowly and thoroughly. They loved until both were breathless.

He rolled off her and cuddled close to her with his arm across her chest and his leg across hers. They lay together in ecstatic silence, drinking in the moment.

The moonlight glimmered around them. Such passion brings such peace.

DAY-6

BACK AT SEA

MORNING DIRECTIVE

As he was accustomed to doing, Frank woke early, before dawn. Debra was still sound asleep next to him. He so wanted to touch her, caress her, hold her, but didn't want to wake her. He lay in bed staring at the ceiling, still amazed at this desire, this passion, this love he had for her. These feelings were so strange and foreign to him that he didn't know what to do. He wasn't sure about them, about her... about him. Was it real? Or did he just want it to be real? All he knew was that when he was with her, he was happier than he had ever been in his entire life. And when he wasn't with her, all he could think about was getting back to her. He regretted that a relationship like this hadn't happen sooner in his life, but he was so happy that it happened now. *Better late than never, old man.*

He crawled out of bed slowly, careful not to wake her. He caught sight of her sheer black nightgown, still lying on the floor where she had eased it from her body last night. Gently he picked it up, held it for a moment, and draped it across the bed where she would see it when she woke. He slipped on his shorts and stepped out onto the balcony. The blackness of the night was giving way to the unearthly gray that signals the approach of dawn. He watched the waves go by as the ship slid through the water with hardly a sound or vibration. Forgetting time, he stayed on the balcony leaning against the rail, thinking.

He had always had a good grasp of his life. It was planned out. He was in control. But now that he loved Debra, all that was gone. The planning and control had been replaced by a single simple desire to be with her. He couldn't imagine his life without her. He wondered whether she felt the same. What would happen tomorrow after they docked? Would all this be written off as a shipboard romance and both of them return to their respective lives as if it never happened? She had said she loved him, over and over, but was it as strong and passionate as his love for her?

The orange tip of the sun climbed out of the sea and he felt a soft touch on his back.

"Beautiful, isn't it?" Debra put her arm across his shoulders.

Frank nodded, slipped his arm around her waist and gently pulled her close to him. She nuzzled his cheek. She wore that soft, luxurious white robe supplied by the ship for each cabin.

"Yes. Amazing. I've seen hundreds of sunrises and sunsets and it never gets old. They never look the same. They are always fascinating... and yes, beautiful."

"You're up early... and dressed."

"Well, sorta dressed. I always get up early. Always have."

"Why don't you come back to bed?" She walked back into her cabin.

He stayed out on the balcony a few moments longer and took another look at the sun before going inside. At the side of the bed he stopped with a gasp. She lay across it with her robe slightly open, smiling up at him.

Every cell in his body cried out for her. He knelt on the floor next to the bed and caressed her feet. Then he kissed her toes, one by one. His hands slowly and softly crept up her legs. He kissed each foot, then her ankles, calves, and knees. She reached for him in loving welcome, but he gently pushed her hands away. He began to kiss her thighs, first the tops and then the outsides. When he moved to the insides, he felt her fingers caressing his hair. He pulled off his shorts and took her just as she climaxed. Fever took them again and they made love with abandonment. The early morning sun bathed the cabin orange as it rose with their passion.

Once again they lay close, spent, entranced, catching their breath.

Frank turned his face toward hers. "This is insane, you know." He paused long enough for Debra to look at him. "I've never felt anything like this in my life. I've never loved anyone like this." He sat up in the bed. "When I'm not with you, all I think about is being close to you. When I'm with you, all I think about is making love to you. Is that sick? The moment I walk out that door, I want to turn right around and come right back. What's wrong with me?"

Tears rose in her eyes. "I don't see anything wrong with that at all. I seem to feel the same way."

"I've never felt like this, Deb. Never. I don't know if it's real or a fantasy." He paused. "This is all so new."

"Are you happy?"

"When I'm with you, yes. When I'm not, I just feel sad." He paused. "Never felt like that. Ever. Didn't know I could." He stood and got dressed, walked to the balcony, picked up his sandals, and headed for the door. He stopped at the door and turned to her, still lying on the bed.

"Honey, where are you going? Did I do something wrong?"

"Nothing is wrong. In fact, it's all perfect." He smiled and looked at the clock on the nightstand. "Okay. It's eight-thirty. You now have one hour to get ready and meet me in the dining hall for breakfast. The attire for the day, and all day, is swimwear. I shall expect you there at nine-thirty." He opened the cabin door and waited in the doorway. "Got it?"

"Swimwear? Like bathing suit swimwear?"

"Exactly."

"Wait a minute, Frank. You have to tell me what we're doing." She sat up in bed and frowned at him. "I have to know which suit to wear. Are we going to be in public?"

He stepped back into the cabin, letting the door close behind him, smiling at the womanly concern on her face.

"Sure. We are going to spend the entire day lounging by the pool."

"Oh, no, Frank. I can't do that. First of all, I can't be in the sun that long. Secondly... Secondly, I have to wear my one-piece suit around people." She quailed a bit under his scolding frown. "This sixty-year-old body doesn't parade around in public."

He chuckled and softly shook his head. He sat down on the edge of the bed and took her hand. "Honey, I would never do anything to upset you. Do you believe that?"

She nodded.

"Good. First of all, you have a magnificent body, regardless of your age. You look thirty. But I understand your apprehension. Secondly, we don't have to be in the sun any more than we want to be."

"I don't understand."

He leaned in and kissed her cheek. He whispered in her ear. "I reserved a cabana for us for the entire day."

"Really? A cabana?"

He nodded. "Yeah. The whole day."

She threw her arms around him. "Wonderful!"

"We can close it up whenever we've had enough of the sun... or the silly public. We can swim when we want, lounge, eat, drink... whatever we want. All day long."

"Oh, Frank. It's perfect."

He took her wrists to remove her arms, stood and went back to the door. "Dining hall, nine-thirty?"

"Nine-thirty. I think I can remember that."

"Good. Oh, and wear your two-piece." He let the door almost close behind him, then flung it back open. "By the way, I love you."

They smiled at each other.

"See you soon."

BY THE POOL

At nine-thirty sharp Debra met him in the dining hall. She wore a white cover-up, sandals, and a large floppy straw hat covering her braided hair. All she needed was big sunglasses to complete the Hollywood glamour look; Frank was certain those were in her matching white bag. She stepped back and surveyed him. He wore sandals, blue-and-white swim trunks, and a light blue sport shirt, topped with a veteran's ball cap.

She shook her head. "Such a slave to fashion."

"Practical, my dear, just practical. Now let's go, my beauty, I'm starving." He offered her his arm and escorted her to a table, where they enjoyed a leisurely breakfast together.

"Before I forget, or in case I forget -- which I will undoubtedly do -- we are in Cabana Number Eight. And that's my lucky number."

"We'll see about that. Number Eight, huh? Got it."

After breakfast they strolled to the adult pool, arm-in-arm and laughing. They found cabana number eight. The flaps were closed. Frank untied the canvas straps and flipped back the flaps. Debra took a step inside and stopped, her hands at her mouth. Her wide eyes and surprised smile made his heart skip a beat.

A large white scented candle, surrounded by carnations, was burning in the center of the side table. A pitcher of iced tea with two glasses sat nearby. Two brightly colored lounge chairs were pushed together to form one large two-person lounger. A bouquet of red, white, and yellow roses stood on a cocktail table beside the lounge chairs, while tulips, lilies, and daisies bloomed on the other.

Debra gazed at her lover, her surprise and happiness barely contained.

"Oh, Frank. This... this is so beautiful. I can't believe you did all this." Tears welled up in her eyes. She put her arms around him and held him close. "You are the sweetest man I have ever met." She kissed his cheek and wiped away a tear.

"I take it you're pleased."

"Oh, honey. This is tremendous. Thank you! I can't believe you did all this."

"Well, have a seat, my dear. Relax. Or we'll swim. Or doze. Whatever you want."

She walked to the roses and smelled them. Their fragrance filled the cabana. She turned to smile at him lovingly as he stood by the entrance watching her. She dropped her bag next to the table of roses and sat down, slipped out of her sandals and reclined on the lounge.

He poured two glasses of iced tea and handed one to her. "How is it?"

"These are very comfortable. I'm pretty sure I can stay here all day."

He removed his shirt and ball cap and looked out over the pool area. She sighed, shivering at the sight of his body. She should be used to seeing it by now, but she wasn't. She wanted him again. He was a magnet for all her senses.

"So. You want to relax for a while? Or do you want to take a swim first?"

She set her iced tea on the table and sat up, smiling at him. "Let's get wet." She stood and removed her cover-up, revealing a modest, pretty, two-piece blue swimsuit. She stepped back into her sandals.

"You are absolutely gorgeous."

"Thanks, honey."

They walked out to the pool, where Debra jumped right in. Frank had to feel his way into the water a little at a time, letting his body get used to the temperature change. He swam to her. Her legs wrapped around his waist, her arms about his shoulders. He held her close by her hips. She kissed him and smiled. Only their heads showed above the water.

"Did you ever make love in a pool?" she asked softly.

He thought about it and smiled back at her. "Actually, not a pool. But I did make love in the ocean once. That was a strange experience." He paused. "Then I made love in a hot tub a couple of times. Never a pool, though. How about you?"

Debra pressed herself against him. "No, never. But there's always a first time."

They kissed gently, with more tenderness than passion. She broke away, laughing from sheer joy, pushed his head underwater and swam away as fast as she could. She expected to feel his hand on her ankle at any second, but she came up for air alone. She brushed her hair out of her eyes and looked around the pool for him, ready to tease him about his slowness.

She spotted him at last, on the other side of the pool, talking to that awful Rhonda and an unfamiliar scrawny redhead. She watched him for a moment to see what would happen. How strange to see him look at, much less talk to, another woman. She had never been the jealous type, but a painful, unfamiliar anger was growing inside her. *I will scratch their eyes out.* How strange —she had never felt that way before. How long would he stand there, not thinking about her for once?

It took her a moment to realize that Frank was scouring the pool with his eyes. When he spotted her, he waved, said a word to the two women, and swam off toward her. By the time he reached her and held her again, she'd forgotten about everything but him.

The day was glorious. They swam and played together, ate a hearty late lunch, napped briefly in each other's arms, got some sun, even joined a pickup game of water polo. Being together was pure delight.

As evening descended, Debra started to feel cold. "Frank, I'm going to run down to my cabin for some warmer clothes. And some lotion – my skin feels like alligator hide. You need anything?"

"No, thanks, sweetie. I'm going to rest here and order us dinner. What do you feel like?"

"Oh, just a salad, thanks. Not very hungry." She thought for a moment. "And a hot-fudge sundae!"

They laughed together. "Don't be gone too long," he said. "I might get lonely."

"Be right back, lover." It was so difficult to pull herself away from him, as he lay there handsome and loving on the lounge chair. His wet swimsuit clung tightly to his skin, leaving little to the imagination. One more loving hug, and then she was off.

SUDDEN CHANGE

Debra got off the elevator and strode to her cabin, humming a silly song they'd sung together in the pool. She showered off the saltwater, combed out her hair, and pulled on chic slacks and a pretty blouse – just the thing to wear while spending the evening with the most wonderful man in the world. She checked messages and listened to an amusing rundown of Becky's day with Paul. Then a question: Would Debra like to invite Frank for a visit after the cruise?

Well. What about him? She sat on the bed for a moment, suddenly sober. The two of them were practically inseparable now, and so happy together – surely this wasn't an empty shipboard romance. They hadn't talked about what would happen after the cruise docked tomorrow, but he must be wondering about that as well. She hoped she wouldn't have to ask him when they could be together again; he must know how much she loved him and wanted to be with him.

She smiled. Maybe making plans for the future was on the menu for this evening, after such a wonderful day. She touched up her makeup and made her way back up to the main deck and cabana number eight. *Heaven on earth.*

The cabana flaps were closed again; no doubt he was tired from the day's exertions and had fallen asleep waiting for her. She looked forward to teasing him about that. She glanced around the pool area. It was mostly empty, since passengers were at dinner or busy packing. Well, it was her turn to surprise him. She began to unbutton her blouse as she drew near.

How strange. Laughter was coming from inside the cabana. She opened the flaps and slipped inside.

Frank lay on their lounge chair. Rhonda sat at his feet and that bony redhead reclined on Debra's side next to him, a goofy smile on her painted mouth. They all turned to stare at her.

"What the hell –"

He scrambled to his feet, his smile vanishing. "Debra!"

She turned and ran from the cabana, fighting back angry tears.

Frank stumbled to the cabana opening and charged out after her. He stopped. There was no sign of her. He turned back and saw Rhonda standing in the opening of the cabana.

"Oh, come on back and lay down for a while, honey. She'll be all right. She just needs to calm down a bit."

"Thanks a lot, Rhonda. You've really done it this time." He shook his head angrily and raced out of the pool area.

Frank listened at Debra's cabin door but didn't hear a sound. He raised his hand to knock sharply, but changed his mind. What would he say? What *could* he say that would explain what she had seen? It was innocent enough. They had just stopped by to say good night but had gotten him into a drawn-out conversation about Dave Sorenson. When Debra came in, she had simply jumped to an incorrect conclusion. *Maybe Rhonda was right, and she needs to settle down before I talk to her.* He slowly and quietly backed away from her door.

He walked down the corridor with his head hung low, feeling terrible. Their beautiful, wonderful day was ruined in a single second of bad judgment. Maybe waiting for her to calm down was the wrong move. He had to explain it to her. He stopped, turned back, and knocked firmly. There was no answer. He listened but heard nothing but silence. He knocked again, harder this time. Still no answer.

"Debra? Please answer. I have to talk to you." He banged harder on the door. "Debra?"

Nothing. Was she sitting there, listening in silence?

He stood outside her door for a few minutes, hoping to hear any sound at all. But there was none. Angry and despondent, he turned away and walked on up to his stateroom. He studied every person he passed in hopes one of them would be Debra.

Back in his room, he walked out to the balcony and looked down on her balcony. No light came from her cabin.

"I guess she isn't there... but where the hell could she be?"

DAVE

Debra was devastated. Seeing Frank with that Rhonda creature and the scrawny redhead had crushed her. She felt used, cheap, rejected, humiliated. She ran down the corridor past the elevators and down the steps to her deck. She stopped. She didn't want to go to her cabin, not where they had made passionate love the night before. She couldn't bear to be there right now.

Tears streamed from her eyes in uncontrollable sobs as she climbed the stairs away from her deck. Two levels later she saw a settee against the wall and sat down wearily. She noticed the sign on the wall: "Empress." Frank's stateroom was on this deck. She jumped back up. She couldn't be seen here.

As she rose, she felt a hand on her shoulder.

"Debra, what's wrong?"

She looked up into Dave Sorenson's hazel eyes. His touch was surprisingly gentle and comforting. More than anything right now she needed gentleness and comforting. She wanted to say something, but all she could do was cry. He sat down next to her and handed her a clean, neatly folded, monogrammed handkerchief. She accepted it without a word.

"Debra? Come on, what is it? What happened?"

"Oh, Dave..." she sobbed, "...I'm sorry. It's not your concern."

"What happened? Was it Frank? What did he do to you?" Dave paused and watched her cry for a moment. "Did he hurt you? I'll kick his ass."

Several people approached. He helped her to her feet, shielding her from their view.

"Looks like the entertainment is letting out. Come on with me, Debra. Let's go somewhere we can talk." With her hand in his and his arm around her shoulder, he guided her down the hallway… toward his stateroom. Debra, still in a daze from her emotions, followed blindly.

He slid his keycard in the door and pushed the door open. She started to walk in and then abruptly stopped. She looked at him and stepped back into the hall.

"No, Dave, I'm not going into your room with you. What are you trying to pull here? This is all I need." She lurched away from him. "Betrayed by someone who I thought loved me, now *you* taking advantage of my emotional state—"

He walked toward her. "You got me all wrong, Deb. Honestly, I'm just trying to help."

"No. You can go to hell."

"Leave the door open. We can stand in the hall if you like." Dave leaned against the doorway. "Believe it or not, I've been where you are. It's no fun. I can honestly say it felt pretty good to talk it out." He smiled at her and waited.

Debra took a calming deep breath. Maybe he was right. "I'm sorry, Dave. Right now, I don't have a very good opinion of your gender as a whole."

"Understandable."

"The door stays open… at all times."

"Absolutely." He picked up a magazine and jammed it under the door, then walked to the table. "I'll fix us a little drink."

Slowly she walked inside, unsure of herself. She half-leaned, half-sat on the dresser close to the door.

Dave handed her a glass and she took a sip. The liquid tasted good but burned a bit as she swallowed. She coughed slightly and looked at him quizzically.

"It's rum, diluted with a little water," he said with a smile. He walked back away from her and sat next to the table on the other side of the cabin. She stayed close to the door.

"Now, tell me. What happened with you and Frank?"

Debra hesitated. She wanted to talk to someone, to tell someone what had happened. But she wasn't sure she wanted to tell him. She took another sip of the rum and stared at him, trying to gauge his sincerity. She briefly wondered what Frank would do if he found her in Dave's stateroom. *It would serve him right. Let him see how it felt to be thrown over.*

Sorenson sat back and kicked off his shoes. "Deb, you don't have to say anything if you don't want to. You can just stay here and relax as long as you want. Whatever you want."

She rose and casually walked to the door to glance up and down the corridor. No Frank. Relieved yet disappointed, she leaned against the door and began telling Dave the story about this evening.

A knock on a door across the hall stopped her voice. She looked out into the hallway and saw a waiter leave Frank's stateroom. She froze. He turned and saw her. Their eyes met. She ducked back in and quickly pulled the door closed.

FRANK

Frank was distraught and angry. He had to find Debra and talk to her, explain the misunderstanding. But he had no idea where she was. Worriedly he paced around his stateroom. It was such a big ship; she could be anywhere.

He'd better calm down. He called room service for a sandwich and two scotches. As he hung up the phone, he had a revelation. "Paul!" It was only logical that she would run to her big brother. He grinned and sat on the bed. He would win back not only his lover, but her family as well. He reached for the phone again.

There was a knock on his door. *Debra?* He opened to the waiter, who set his food and drink on the table. He escorted the man to the door, tipped him and signed the check, casually glancing up and down the corridor. His eyes stopped on a beautiful woman holding a drink and standing in the doorway of Dave's stateroom. His eyes widened.

"Debra?!"

She dashed back inside and closed the door.

"What the hell...?" Frank charged out of his stateroom and stormed toward Dave's, but stopped halfway there. *What the hell's going on? What's she doing in that bastard's room?*

Then he had a thought. He smiled bitterly. "Okay, Debra," he mumbled as he turned back to his room. "I know your little game." She was obviously going to try to get even with him and get him as mad and jealous as she was about Rhonda and What's-her-name. So, she was with Dave. Women! They were all alike.

Frank crept quietly back to his room. He paced, he sat, he sipped his scotch, he paced some more. He was torn between needing to talk with her and explain -- and despising her little jealousy game... even though the thought of her being anywhere near that creep was driving him crazy.

But maybe he was wrong. Maybe she wasn't playing a game. Maybe she needed his help.

He sat down again and picked at his sandwich. He'd lost his appetite. He tossed back the rest of his first drink and started angrily on the second, pacing again. The thought of her with Sorenson was eating at him. His jealousy raged inside him to the point where he couldn't take it anymore. He flung open his door and marched to Dave's cabin, where he pounded on the door. It opened and there stood Barbie.

"Ooohhh, it's Frankie! Hi, good-lookin'! You're just the person we need to make this party worthwhile. Come on in, sweetie."

Frank stared at her, astonished. He looked inside and saw Dave sitting at the table and Rhonda lying across the bed. Both women grinned at him invitingly. He took a step back. Had he really seen Debra, or had he seen one of them and just imagined her to be Debra? *I must be losing my mind.* Neither of them resembled her in the slightest.

"Sorry," he stammered. "I... didn't know... I'd better go." He was back in the corridor when Dave came out and stopped him.

"Hey, Frank. Debra was here a few minutes ago. She's really upset."

Frank stared at Dave with a little fire in his eyes.

"We just talked, okay? Nothing happened. You can get that notion out of your head right now. She's obviously nuts about you, dummy. You need to talk with her and work this out. But I'd wait till morning if I was you." He paused. "That's my advice – but, hell, what do I know? I've ended up with these two broads." He slipped back inside. "Good luck, pal."

Frank stood alone in the empty corridor, his mind awhirl. Those two scotches hadn't helped at all. Maybe he needed a third and a fourth. He stopped at his stateroom, but didn't go in. Maybe Dave was right. Maybe he should let this simmer overnight and talk with her in the morning. He just couldn't face her – and her brother – right now.

He walked up to the main deck and sat down at the closest bar and ordered a scotch. Other than a few couples having a late dinner, the place was empty. But something about it looked familiar... It was the restaurant where he and Debra had shared their first dance.

Another drink. As he took his first sip, music began to play in the background. Again he felt her light, smooth, sweet, supple body in his arms. He brushed sudden moisture from his eyes and signaled for a third.

DAY-7

DISEMBARKING

LEAVING

Listlessly Debra checked over her carry-on bag one more time as she listened to the disembarking instructions on the ship's television. Returning to the home dock was always the saddest part of a trip... and without Frank it was doubly sad. Her week long cruise was over. She slipped some money into an envelope for the steward and his staff, and slowly went through all the drawers and closets one more time. She wanted to cry again, but felt she was all cried out. She was riding an emotional rollercoaster of depression, regret, anger, sadness... passionate love. Was it gone? Was it ever really there?

There it was, at the back of the drawer where she'd kept her jewelry; the silver shell she'd pulled from underneath herself in the warm sand that day. That day she'd been so sure of their love.

She moved slowly to the balcony one last time, gazing at the shell. She stretched out her hand as if to toss it into the sea, back where it belonged. But it was so beautiful and so rare. She couldn't help but smile in wonder.

But it also brought the thought of Frank. *How could he be like other men: callous, untrue, ready to leap from one woman to another?*

She went back into her cabin and gently placed the shell on the desk. The next guests would find it and wonder about it. *Maybe they would find true love. Maybe it was meant for them, not me.*

Maybe the steward would just sling it into the trash...

She shook herself and glanced one last time at the cabin telephone. No word from Frank. Well, to be fair, the message light was blinking. There had been a couple of calls, but she hadn't had the strength to answer them or listen to the messages. She still was in no mood to be rational.

She leaned against the little desk, emptily thinking over the past week. Such happiness – and then, in an instant, such dismay. She felt weak and disoriented from a sleepless, mournful night. The emptiness of a future without him yawned before her.

Oh, the irony, she thought. *I started this cruise grieving for Tom, and I leave it mourning the loss of Frank.* It was corny, yes, but still she wondered how she could live without him.

She stood wearily and leaned down to pick up her bag, then angrily stomped her foot and slammed the bag back down on the bed. *Why the hell didn't he come after me last night?* She sat down again, full of questions. Did she overreact? Should she have stayed in the cabana and confronted them all? Those horrid women.

Oh, why didn't he come?

Sadness welled up in her like a volcano. She burst into tears once more and fell back onto the bed and cried into her pillow.

A knock on the cabin door threw her into confusion and a reckless hope. "Frank!" She raced to the door and was about to launch herself into his arms, but stopped short. "Oh. It's you."

"Well. How do you like that welcome?" Paul said to Becky. "It's real good to see you, too, Sis."

"I'm sorry, Paul. I didn't mean it that way." She sat back down on the bed and lowered her head. He set his carry-on bag down and sat next to her.

"Hey, hey, what is this? What's wrong, honey? Something is. I can tell." He put his arm around her shoulder and pulled her close. Becky, quiet for once, sat down on the other side and took her hand.

"Frank and I had a… a… Oh, what's the use?" She stood up. "I was hoping he would come by this morning, or at least call. We ended last night on some rather bad terms."

"What happened?" Paul asked. "What did he do to you?"

"It wasn't Frank, Paul. He... was... he didn't do anything. It was me. I was being an idiot. Again. That's what happened."

"Let me guess... You overreacted and jumped to the wrong conclusion."

"Well, why would you think – ? Oh... Have I always been this way, Paul?"

"Yep." He got up and put his arms around his sister and kissed her gently on her forehead. "That's why you could never hold on to a guy you were dating very long. You made assumptions about what they were doing or not doing or should be doing, and then reacted on your assumptions. Usually by getting mad at them for something they never did. Not healthy, Sis."

"Oh, shut up."

"So, you sat up crying all night waiting for Frank to call or come crawling back here begging you to take him back."

She didn't answer.

"Right? Why didn't you answer the phone?" Paul paused. "Why didn't you call him?"

Debra looked surprised. "Did he call? How would you know I didn't answer it?"

"Because I called this morning and you didn't answer." He walked to the phone. "And, duh, the message light is blinking."

She stared at him. "Did you leave that message?"

"I left one of them."

"How do you know there's more than one?"

"How do you know there isn't?" He picked up the receiver and handed it to her. Then he pressed the message button. "Let's find out."

She listened to her brother's message and a little smile crept to her face.

"There, Debra, you see?" Becky scolded her lovingly.

They listened on. There was another call but no message. Then there was another message. From Frank. He apologized and went on and on about his love for her. She could tell he had been drinking, but she could also tell he had been crying. Tears welled as she hung up.

"So. Apparently there was a message from Frank. What did he say?"

"He was drinking." She looked down and lowered her voice. "He said he loved me."

"Oh. So, this monster who never loved you and just used you for his sexual satisfaction all week long actually called you? Why? Not to curse you, but to profess his lifelong adoration for you." Paul turned to his wife dramatically. "What do you think, Becky? Doesn't that sound like a horrible man?"

"Okay, Paul, I get it." Debra sat on the bed. "Well, I guess I did it again." She quickly stood back up with a sudden revelation. "I've got to see him." She picked up her bag, but Paul stopped her.

"Empress Deck disembarked hours ago, Sis. I'm afraid he's gone."

Debra sank back down on the bed and wept, not caring whether they saw her. Paul strolled onto the balcony as Becky cradled her in her arms.

"I love him, Paul."

"I know, honey."

Soon they all heard the announcement for the Venetian Deck to disembark. It was time to go. Debra composed herself, stood up, and shook off her hopelessness best she could. She put on her darkest sunglasses and tied a silk scarf around her long hair. She picked up her carry-on bag and stepped out into the hallway with Paul and Becky. She cast a final look into her cabin and her eyes came to rest on her bed. She recalled the amazing lovemaking she had shared with Frank in that bed.

Then her eyes drifted to the silver shell. She reached for it but had second thoughts. Her own words to Kim before the cruise came back to her *"...what use would I have for a silver shell at my age?"*

It was really over. Silent tears flowed as she let the cabin door click behind her for the last time.

PLOTTING

Frank spent the better part of the night nursing a headache and wallowing in self-pity. *Why did I drink so much?* He tried to sleep but couldn't get Debra out of his mind. Not that he wanted to. He thought a few drinks might help, but they just intensified his misery. He loved her. He needed her. Sometime in the middle of the night, and before he sobered up entirely, he called her. She wisely didn't answer. He had left a message but wasn't sure exactly what he said. He remembered calling again without bothering to leave a message. He'd surely messed things up even worse by doing all that.

All night long he would run out to his balcony and look down on hers, hoping to catch a glimpse of her. Sometimes her light was on, sometimes it was off. She must have had a restless sleep too. He'd called room service and fallen into bed.

Now he sat at his table drinking coffee and eating the sweet rolls, trying to come up with a plan to run into her. He really wanted to go down and knock on her door, but he couldn't deal with any more rejection from her. No, he would just have to run into her and catch her off-guard. He had to tell her how he felt, how much she meant to him, how much he loved her. *If she doesn't want to see me, then at least I'll know. I'll know how she feels.*

Frank left the ship as soon as the gangway was opened to departing passengers. He had packed last night and made sure his luggage was first to be picked up. He had to watch every person disembarking. He couldn't miss Debra. He had to talk to her. He even went by her cabin.

On his way off the ship he passed through the duty-free shopping area and stopped at the florist. All the stores on the ship were closed, but she was still inside doing inventory.

Frank tried the door, but it was locked. He knocked on the window. The florist shook her head and mouthed the word "Closed." He knocked again. She turned away with a phony little smile. He pressed a hundred-dollar bill against the glass and knocked harder.

"Yes, sir, what is it? We're getting ready for the new passengers."

"I'm sorry to bother you, but you can help me save the love of my life."

"But, sir, a hundred dollars? I really shouldn't—"

"If this works, it'll be worth it."

Inside the cruise terminal, Frank parked himself at a good vantage point. And he waited.

ENCOUNTER

Debra strode down the gangway with Paul and Becky. On the way they ran into the Tates, the children frothing around her in their eagerness to be going home. As she watched them and listened half-heartedly to their chatter, she mentally turned the key of her own front door. She just could not picture herself going into the empty house, not with the desolate heart she carried. Well, it would only be empty for a little while – Kim would join her soon to finish planning the wedding. She could not bring herself to care even the slightest about that. She would have to deal with that later.

Annie Tate pulled at her slacks and talked incessantly. Debra pretended to listen but all the while her eyes scanned the crowd hoping to catch a glimpse of Frank.

Her parents shushed her and pulled her away gently. "Sorry, Miss Debra."

She smiled. "Oh, she's fine. I don't mind in the least."

"Is Frank coming off with you?" Mrs. Tate asked. "He was certainly a nice man. I liked him a lot."

"So did I." She looked away. "So did I."

"Well, goodbye and take care. It was lovely meeting you."

"Goodbye!"

Once they were all outside the port and everyone had claimed their luggage, Paul helped Debra put her bags into a taxi for the airport.

"Aren't you coming to the airport?"

"No, not today. We decided to take a shuttle to the hotel. We're going to stay the night and fly back home tomorrow. It's so hectic having all that travel in one day, so we spend the night and unwind a little. Becky will have to repack all the crap she bought. Then we'll go back home at our leisure."

"That's a very smart plan. I was just hoping for a little more time with you two."

"Why don't you stay the night, Debra?" Becky coaxed. "Unwind with us and we'll all go back together."

Debra smiled and hugged her sister-in-law in newfound affection. "That sounds nice, but I don't think I can change my tickets. Thanks, anyway."

"You okay, Debs?"

"Yes, Paul. Thank you for a wonderful cruise."

They all hugged and exchanged promises to call when they got back home. With a brittle smile she waved them off to their shuttle, then turned miserably once more to look toward the ship. *Can it really end this way, after all that love?* Apparently, it could.

She sighed and turned toward the taxi. She was about to get in when a perfect yellow rose appeared before her eyes.

"Debra."

His voice struck her heart like music.

"Listen, driver, I may be going to the airport with this lady. But please just give us a minute." Frank handed his bags to the cabby and took Debra by the hand. "Come and talk with me, just for a minute. I'm sure you hate me right now, but give me just one last moment. Please?"

She longed for the comfort and strength of his arms but was afraid of what he had to say. She stood firmly for a moment but then followed him as he led her away from the cab. She didn't know how to feel.

They walked to a nearby bench under some trees. "Sit down. Please."

She stood indecisively for a moment, then did as he asked. She was too tired and too emotionally drained to resist.

"You didn't answer my calls last night. I was on my way to your cabin to explain..."

"You were drinking. I wasn't going to talk to you in that state."

"But you didn't know that when I called. You must have listened to my message. Didn't that mean anything to you? When I –"

He looked away, overcome by emotion. She looked up at him for a moment.

"It's all right, Frank, I... I really do understand. On your way to my cabin, you realized that there was nothing between us and you didn't want to bother explaining about your friends."

He turned to her angrily. "Is that what you thought? That I didn't care? That our love... that what happened between us this week was just one of those damned shipboard romances? I didn't think you would."

"It's all right, Frank," she repeated woodenly. "We had a wonderful time and, yes, I loved you. I thought you loved me. I was so happy with you. But if it was just one of those things, we wouldn't be the first."

"It wasn't," he said fiercely. "Not for me. And you were certainly convincing that it wasn't for you."

Her face felt hot. She got wearily to her feet and started for the taxi. "What's the difference, Frank? You're a free man. You can go and do what you want. With whoever you want."

He grabbed her arm and whirled her around to face him. "Wait a minute. I come to you with my heart in my hands and you pull this tough-girl act? I was tearing my hair out all night long thinking I'd lost you. Well, did I? Did I lose you?"

He paused, but she didn't answer.

"Even though I didn't do anything wrong, I'm here to beg your forgiveness. I'm having a hard time trying to figure out why you're so mad. Can you explain it to me?"

Debra realized she wasn't angry anymore.

"And another thing. What the hell were you doing in Dave's room last night?"

She looked deep into his eyes as a slight smile crept to one corner of her mouth. *He's jealous. He really does care.* "Oh, that. Well... he just sort of came by when I was standing at your door... and... uh... well... Nothing."

"You came to my door?" Roughly he pulled her sunglasses away, making her wince in the sunlight. "Listen to me. I love you, Debra. More than I've ever loved any woman. I meant every word I said to you on this trip, in bed and out of it. You are wonderful, and... and I love you passionately. Do not let it end this way. Please. I'm begging you."

Her lips trembled. "But... what about—"

"Those women? They just stopped by to say goodnight. They hoped to see you too. They didn't know you were gone. We just got to talking, is all. She'd just seen me at the pool earlier and wanted to say goodbye in case we didn't run into each other again."

"Looked pretty friendly to me."

"Don't be stupid. I couldn't stand her and her idiot friend – all I wanted was to be with you. But you walked in and apparently came to some conclusion that – I don't know what. I guess maybe it looked pretty bad. I'm sorry. I'm sorry, sweetheart! *Nothing* happened. Nothing was ever *going* to happen. It's you and only you that I love. Please don't let it end... not like this."

Debra held the yellow rose to her face, inhaling its sweet calming fragrance.

"On the way to your cabin last night, my own insecurities snuck up on me. I knocked. I knocked a couple of times. I figured you didn't answer because you didn't want to see me. I thought you didn't care enough to believe me. Enough to laugh it off. Enough to wait for an explanation. Enough maybe even to be a little..." His voice trailed off in embarrassment.

"A little what, Frank? Jealous? I'm ashamed that that's what it was. That, and all my fears that it wasn't real. That you'd been playing with me for a week. That we'd part today and never see each other again..."

"Tell me, Debra. What do you want? In your heart, what do you really want?"

The rose smelled even sweeter now.

"I want you, Frank."

He coughed a smile from a sob. "All I want is you. You're my everything. I couldn't live without your love."

They stood looking at each other, unaware of anything else.

The blast of the ship's horn made them both jump. Simultaneously they moved into each other's arms.

"Were you jealous, really? That's wonderful."

"I love you, Frank." She kissed his lips and then smiled at him. "Now, tell me what you were thinking when you saw me in Dave's room." Her smile widened.

"Okay, yes. I was furious. Crazy with jealousy. Happy now? I wanted to go over there and kick his ass."

"What stopped you?"

"I thought... well, I just thought that..." He paused and looked into her eyes. "You're enjoying me squirming, aren't you?"

"Oh, yes. Very much. Go on, please, what stopped you?"

"Let's just say I came to my senses. I'd already hit him once on this trip. If I did it again, I'd be in jail. Besides, I love you, too."

"So it's real?"

He kissed her.

"Yes."

She took his proffered arm and they walked slowly back to the taxi.

"To the airport, please."

On the way they sat together thinking about the future. It was going to be difficult to see each other as often as they would like. Right now, they were content in each other's arms.

"Ever make love in the back seat of a car?" he whispered.

Debra giggled and blushed, snuggling closer to him. They rode in rapturous silence.

DAY-7

AIRPORT

GOODBYE

At the airport Frank helped Debra check her luggage, then they wound their way through Security together. They were travelling to different cities in different parts of the country on different airlines. The harsh reality of their relationship slid bitterly into focus. They stopped and stood a step apart in the crowded airport.

"So..." Frank muttered.

"Yeah. So...."

"When's your flight?"

Debra glanced sadly at the digital clock on the wall. "It's boarding in about an hour." She stared lovingly at him, locking on to those hypnotic blue eyes. "When's yours?"

He glanced at his wristwatch. "I got a few hours, yet. No hurry." He held her in his eyes, wanting to grab her and love her once more. Then he looked away.

"This is impossible, isn't it?"

Surprised, he jerked his head back to look at her. He opened his mouth to contradict her, but there was nothing there. It was impossible, and he knew it too. "What are you talking about?" he asked, not very convincingly.

"Sweetie, I've never loved anyone like I love you. I've never been loved by anyone the way you love me."

"Well, then, what's the problem?"

"The problem is pretty obvious, don't you think?" She moved a bit farther away. "You're flying west and I'm flying north. You're flying back to life after a broken marriage of forty years. It's your reality and a very different life away from that ship... a life I have no part in. I'm flying back to a little family that's still trying to pick up the pieces of losing a husband and a father. It's a life with my daughter and her wedding and her new married life and—"

"And a life I have no business in," he finished for her. He lowered his head. "Okay, I get it. I always thought anything was possible, especially with the way we feel about each other. I guess it isn't." He turned away from her.

"Frank..."

"So, this is it? This is goodbye?" He faced her again. "This week meant the world to me, Debra. Didn't it mean anything to you?"

"Oh, Frank, it meant more to me than you could ever know. But, honey, what's the point?" She shook her head. "We live in different parts of the country with different lives ahead of us when we get back. Are you going to leave everything you have back home and come to be with me?"

As much as he wanted to say yes, he couldn't. Not now, anyway. Maybe someday in the future, but he still had the loose ends of his divorce and all the money problems to deal with. His friends and family wouldn't understand. As much as they wanted him to be happy, they wouldn't understand him loving someone new this soon after the divorce.

She watched the emotions chase one another across his honest face. "You see, don't you? Let's face the facts, honey. I can't come and join you, either. I have a family that I can't just up and leave. And to be honest, I don't think they would be too receptive to me bringing you into our lives right now."

"So, this is it? Goodbye at the airport?"

"No, honey. This week was heaven. Telling you all this is breaking my heart. But I don't see how our relationship can work." She paused. "Do you? Long-distance relationships are almost always impossible. I want a solution to how we can keep our love alive. I don't ever want to lose this."

He stood silently, hands jammed into his pockets.

"So tell me how, Frank. Because I have to catch my flight."

He looked suddenly surprised, then drew his right hand out. He took her left hand and pressed something into it.

"Oh, Frank."

It was the silver shell, sleek and luminous. She stared at it, mesmerized by joy and sorrow.

"I went by your cabin one last time but you were gone. The steward let me in. When I saw that you'd left this on the desk I really thought it was over."

They stared helplessly at each other. Tears streamed down her cheeks as she stepped forward into his arms.

"I love you, Frank Watson. I always will... everlasting."

He grabbed her as she started to pull away from him and kissed her. She wrapped her arms around him. The passion flared up in them both again, but soon he broke off the kiss and held her tightly. Passionately, yes, but oh so tender.

"I love you, too, Debra. Everlasting."

They kissed again. He stepped away from her, his arms falling to his sides. "You'd better go, then. You'll miss your plane."

She caressed his face once more and backed away from him, blinking to bring his watery image into focus. She smiled wryly.

"Have a safe trip."

"I'll be in touch."

"You'd better be." She took another step away, then stopped and called impulsively, "Want to come to a wedding?"

He smiled and shrugged, suddenly happier. "I'm pretty busy, you know. But have Kim send me an invitation. We'll see."

He stood gazing at her as she walked away. *So lovely.*

DEBRA

The hardest thing she had ever done was turn around and walk away from him. She couldn't hold back any longer and sobbed. Clutching the silver shell in one hand, she pulled a tissue from her purse with the other and covered her mouth to soften the sobs as she made her way down the corridor toward her gate. She was suddenly conscious of all the people around her.

"Are you all right, miss?" a porter asked.

Debra stopped and looked at him. She nodded and let out a final sob. "Just saying goodbye to someone very special."

"I got you." His gentle smile eased her sadness a bit. "Is there anything I can do?"

"Maybe. Can you make time go backwards?"

The porter chuckled. "I've been looking for some way to do that all my life."

She smiled.

"That's good, ma'am. You're smiling. Things aren't always as bleak as they seem, you know. They usually have a way of workin' out for the best."

She wiped her eyes. "I hope so. But right now I don't see how that's possible. Thank you." She walked on toward her gate.

Suddenly the hairs on the back of her neck stood up. Surely Frank was following her. She spun around to stare back down the wide corridor, wanting so badly to see him. She waited, still staring, for a while. But no Frank. She shook her head. *He's not coming. What are you doing, idiot?* She resumed her trek to the gate.

But it was strange. She couldn't shake the feeling that he wanted her, needed her, was calling to her. She should run right back to his arms -- but she knew she couldn't. Maybe in time. Maybe they would find each other down the road. Maybe she'd take a trip out west. Yes. Maybe he'd visit her. *Maybe, maybe, maybe.*

At the gate she found a seat where she could look down the hall, still desperately hoping he would appear. She gazed at the shell as she relived their goodbyes over and over in her mind, trying to convince herself that it was the right thing to do and the right time to do it. But if it was so right, then why was she so miserable? If she was so confident in her decision, why was she looking down an endless empty hallway for the lover she had just left?

"Attention, please. We will begin boarding shortly." Everyone in the gate area stood and jockeyed for position in the line to board the aircraft.

Everyone except Debra. She had a reserved seat on the plane, didn't she? She would wait till the last possible minute, just in case. She closed her eyes and held the shell tighter with both hands.

FRANK

Frank felt like his life was over. His knees weakened with each step she took away from him. He sat down and thought about what he was losing. How could this be happening? His world surely felt as if it was ending. He would go after her, grab her, take her back to the dock and get on another cruise. It was the only place they could be together, a world separate from their real lives. A place where the outside world couldn't touch them. No phones, no mail or e-mail, no ex-wives and lawyers, no daughters with wedding plans, no...

"You and your fantasy."

He looked around at the cold, grey, impersonal airport walls and the hundreds of strangers scurrying from one point to another. Public address announcements echoed through the aisles in the background. A hapless dog yapped from its little carrier.

He frowned and took a deep breath. "This is reality."

He stood, grabbed his luggage, and began walking to the check-in counter for his airline. He felt a sudden thrill. He stopped and turned around, hoping to see Debra walking toward him. He stared for a long time, but she wasn't there. The one woman in the world who made him happy.

He grimaced at his foolishness. *That kind of crap only happens in movies.*

He stood in a long line at the check-in counter, the feeling of loss growing into physical pain. He gazed back down the terminal in her direction, wishing madly for her to appear. He thought about the life he was going back to: the ex-wife, the lawyers, the finance people, the court people, the headaches, his disappointed son. And the loneliness.

What's the rush to get back to all that? Maybe Debra was right. Maybe her family and friends wouldn't accept him or welcome him. Maybe there was no chance for their separate lives to become one.

Suddenly a thought jumped into his mind. He could always exchange his tickets for a different flight. A later flight. Maybe tomorrow... or even the next day. How could it hurt?

He stepped out of line. She was waiting for him, standing in her own long lonely line, waiting for him to come running down the hallway toward her. Wanting him, sharing his pain. He glanced at his watch. She hadn't boarded yet. She was looking for him. He could feel it.

He rushed from one end of the infinite terminal to the other, dodging people and praying she hadn't boarded yet. No, no, there she was, the next to last one in line, slowly handing her boarding pass to the gate agent.

"Debra!"

She spun around. A light ignited inside her and she smiled... the widest, happiest smile she had ever worn.

"Wait. Don't get on the plane. Please."

"We have to finish boarding now, ma'am." The agent was polite, yet firm.

Debra kept her eyes on Frank as she pulled her boarding pass back.

"Go right ahead. I'm not going. I gate-checked my bag, could you have someone pull it? Please."

The woman looked at her, then at Frank, then back at her. Her expression morphed from professional to human. "Give me a minute." Another agent took her place and she disappeared down the gangway.

Debra was already back in Frank's arms. She couldn't speak. All she could do was laugh.

"I love you, Deb. I can't let you go. Let's have lunch. We'll spend the day together. I'll get us a hotel for the night, and we'll talk. We'll talk about our lives, our plans, Kim's wedding, my divorce. We'll talk about reality, not the fantasy cruise we were just on. What do you say?" He paused for a moment and saw her smile. "We'll work it out. I know we can, honey. You mean too much to me not to. You're everything."

"Oh, Frank, that would mean the world to me. But I can't exchange my ticket."

"I'll get you a new ticket. For tomorrow... or the next day. Say yes! Let's spend some time together in the real world talking about us. The real, live, normal, everyday us. Our future in the real world."

She nodded joyously. "Wonderful. We'll start all over on dry land."

The gate agent returned and handed her the bag. "You're all set, Ms. Dawson. Best wishes." She smiled briefly and ushered the last passenger into the gangway, closing the door behind her.

They stood at the big windows, watching the plane pull away from the gate. Debra sighed.

"Honey?"

"I'm scared, Frank."

"It'll be okay. You'll see, we can make this work. I know we can."

They held each other close and watched the plane taxi away. Together they left the gate, their arms pressed together as they walked. There was no hurry now.

In the concourse he motioned for her to sit down. "You need to call your daughter and tell her you'll be coming in tomorrow. I'm going to rent us a car. Will you stay with me tonight? Or would you prefer a separate room?"

"I must be with you, Frank."

She pulled her cell phone from her purse, surprised to see that her hands were shaking. Her smile faded as she stared at Kim's number.

"You okay?"

"Can you believe this? I'm a little nervous about this. I don't know what I'm going to say to my own daughter."

Frank sat down next to her. "Well, I've always felt the truth is the best thing. However, in this case, the truth will probably require a long, *long* conversation that would be better in person."

She looked at him, perplexed.

"I overheard Paul say they were staying the night to unwind. Didn't he invite you to do the same?"

"Yes, he did."

"Well, say that, if you like. You can tell her the whole truth when you get home. Or you could just –"

"Tell her now?"

His smile said everything.

Debra tapped the Call icon.

"Hi, Mom! Back safe and sound?"

"Hi, honey. I sure am. How are you?"

"Fantastic! We got so many things done for the wedding. But I really missed you. How was the cruise?"

She took Frank's hand. "I had the most wonderful time."

"Did you? That's great! I can't wait to hear all about it."

They smiled at each other. It was going to be all right.

"And, Kim, dear, you'll never guess what happened."

* * * *

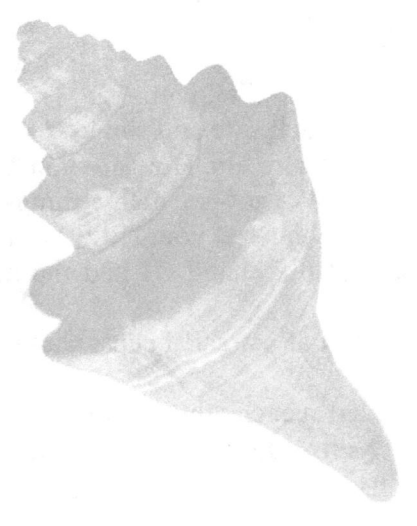

AUTHOR

Deena Logan was born on the East Coast, educated in the Midwest, and currently resides out West. She has been single, married, divorced, and widowed. She's 23, 48, and 72 years old. She is the single-mother waitress in Cleveland, the retired music teacher in Phoenix, the middle-aged office worker in New York, the farm worker just outside of Fresno. Deena is all women, everywhere, who love and want to be loved. She's the heartbroken women who lost a love and thought they would never love again. She's the women in a loveless relationship with little or no hope. She's the lonely woman who sees everyone else in a relationship and lives in the despair of never finding a love of her own. But Deena is hope.

Deena is also the women who are happily in a relationship with the love of their life. She's the women who live everyday loving life and reveling in the things that makes her happy; her children, her career, her friends, and her lovers. Deena is love.

Deena is the guy who is truly looking for a friend, companion, lover, and confidant. Someone who doesn't subscribe to the tough-guy, he-man, macho image of men generated by movies, novels and mass-media. Someone who has, or is looking for, a partner whom he can care for and share his life with. Deena is a person who wants that special someone who sets their soul ablaze and fuses them together.

Deena is all love, hope, desire and passion. And she wants to impart that to all. Love is out there... and it's available to everyone. Yes, everyone. Be open, be free, and don't be afraid to take a chance.

Watch for Deena's next release;

DEENA LOGAN'S ADULT BEDTIME STORIES.

A collection of intimate short love stories strictly for adults.

Scheduled for release in early 2020

Deena would love to hear comments from you and would also love to hear your story of love. You may contact her via email at: deenaloganllc@gmail.com
Or by regular mail at:
P.O. Box 12578
Prescott, AZ 86304

www.ingramcontent.com/pod-product-compliance
Lightning Source LLC
Chambersburg PA
CBHW032138170626
46808CB00006B/2289